Content Note

There is a word in this book that might be difficult for some readers. It's a derogatory name for a gay man.

I've had teachers, colleagues and strangers call me that name. I'm sure I heard it almost every day at school. For me and so many of the gay men I know, this word is part of the experiences that shaped who we are. We all have stories of how it was used to belittle, humiliate or torture us in one way or another. I wanted to bring my authentic self to this book in a way that answered Carina Adores's call for authenticity. I can't deny that this word is part of my reality as a gay man.

In *The Hideaway Inn*, I wanted to write a character who is so shaped by his experience as a teen that he pushes himself in an entirely different direction—only to find out that he's also pushing away the love of his life. That word is part of Vince's experience and it's part of mine. Fortunately, Vince and I have both learned to grow beyond the boxes in which we were placed early in life.

My editor and I had multiple serious and thoughtful conversations about the word in question. She was concerned readers would have difficulty reading it in the context of an endearing romance. I was grateful to hear her thoughts but felt it was important, especially in this context, to destroy the word's power through the story of a transformational love that makes the HEA of *The Hideaway Inn* that much more H. I hope you will agree.

THE HIDEAWAY INN

Philip William Stover

carina
press

**carina
press®**

Recycling programs
for this product may
not exist in your area.

ISBN-13: 978-1-335-14693-9

The Hideaway Inn

Carina Press
22 Adelaide St. West, 40th Floor
Toronto, Ontario M5H 4E3, Canada
www.CarinaPress.com

Printed in U.S.A.

Dear Reader,

I first came to know New Hope, Pennsylvania, as a young kid performing in a summer stock production of *The Wizard of Oz* at the Bucks County Playhouse. (See my website for proof and embarrassing photos.) We rehearsed in a studio with sweeping views of the Delaware River, and between performances I poked around the quaint shops and strolled along the canal path that cut through this idyllic town. I knew I was in a special place, but I was too young to immediately understand why I felt so comfortable.

For decades queer people and allies have found a "hideaway" in this small town and its environs halfway between Philadelphia and New York. Oscar Hammerstein wrote some of the world's most beloved musicals in Bucks County, and Dorothy Parker took a break from the Algonquin Round Table at her country home by the Delaware. In the '60s and '70s, the mainstream press coverage of "Mother Cavallucci's" gay weddings signaled to the world that New Hope was a place of inclusivity.

Despite the allure this area has always held for me, I never thought I would write a gay romantic series set in New Hope. As a young gay boy, reading romance was a way to experiment with love, even if I never saw myself in the pages. But like many experiments, reading romance was also dangerous. I was constantly teased for carrying around my "girly books," so I learned to tear off the covers and read alone in a forgotten, dark corner of the school library.

I'm thrilled to be reembracing my passion for romance. I couldn't be prouder to be one of the launch authors for Carina Adores. Their commitment to inclusivity has given me and others a voice in a genre that I thought lived behind a castle wall. After years of swimming the moat, being welcomed across the drawbridge is exhilarating.

I'm so grateful you are open to reading the first book in my Seasons of New Hope series. I'd love to know what you think. Please find me on social media or visit me at my website: www.philipwilliamstover.com. I've waited a long time to meet you, dear reader, and I hope we can share many happy endings and read together in the sunshine.

Philip William Stover

THE HIDEAWAY INN

For my great romance, WBC.

Chapter One

"This isn't New Hope," I tell the bus driver.

"No, it's Pittstown. Last stop."

Back in Manhattan a company chauffer takes me wherever I need to go but I do pass by plenty of bus stops—little huts with glass walls and cologne ads. Those are bus stops. This isn't a bus stop. It's a cow pasture.

The driver opens the door and the smell of manure is so strong I have to hold the pocket square from my suit jacket over my mouth to stop from gagging.

"Memorial Day weekend schedule. Bus doesn't go all the way to New Hope. Last stop is here, Pittstown."

I look out the window. Cows to the right, empty fields to the left and nothing ahead of me or behind. Dark clouds gather in the sky, threatening an early summer rainstorm.

My first thought is to just throw some money at the guy and bark at him to do what I want but those days are on pause, at least for now.

"Come on, man. My phone's dead. Call an Uber for me?" At this point I'm almost whining, something I never do, but I've been doing a lot of things I never do lately.

"We don't have Uber. You aren't from around here?" He examines me over his sunglasses.

The truth is, I grew up about twenty miles away in a town where the Jersey suburbs rubbed up against the Garden State farmlands. Everything east of that was big box stores and gas stations, everything west was rolling farmland. I pretty much spent my childhood reading overly sentimental verse or searching online for an acne cure.

"No, I'm not."

"There's a general store about six miles ahead. They might be able to call you a cab."

I grab my shoulder bag, thank the guy—for what, I don't know—and step off the bus straight into a puddle of mud. The bus releases its brakes with a hiss of air and then disappears over the hill. I'm alone on the side of the road wearing a three-thousand-dollar bespoke suit and nine-hundred-dollar shoes, covered in mud.

After walking over a mile without passing any living thing except a number of cows who I swear give me dirty looks, a pickup truck zooms past me on a blind curve only to pump the brakes when a bale of hay falls off the back. This could be my ticket out of my misery. With any luck this hick will be a serial killer and he'll see the word *next* written all over me. If that doesn't work out I guess I could ask him to take me to the general store.

I start jogging toward the truck but as the guy steps out, I stop immediately. He's far away but I can see that he is no stranger to hard labor. He's wearing jeans so tight even from this distance I can see that each cheek of his bubble butt is a perfectly proportioned independent entity. Even though it's a chilly sunless day he has his flannel shirt tied around his waist so his tank top reveals sun kissed arms that are thick from what I imagine to be hours of work in the fields. A trucker hat and sunglasses cover his face but that body is enough to turn this whole day around.

I pick up my pace and walk toward the truck. The guy throws a rope around the hay bales in the cargo bed and moves to the other side to secure them.

"Excuse me," I say, and my deep voice booms across the field. I know the effect it usually has on people. At the firm, it made people follow my orders and in bed it does the same thing. It may be a polished performance, but it has great effect.

"Hold up," he says from the other side of the truck. His voice is deep but not as heavy as mine and with less gravel. I hear him fiddling with the rope and can see the hair on his toned arms glisten in the late morning sunlight. I'm already picturing a handsome boyish face with a wide confident smile. I hear the ground crunch under his feet as he walks toward my side of the truck.

He takes one look at me and stops. "No way!" he says. He pulls off his hay-dusted sunglasses. "Skinny Vinny. What the hell are you doing here?"

My body freezes. I can't believe who I'm seeing. It's been over fifteen years, but the sight of him has me feeling like the skinny geeky kid with the impossible crush.

I quickly gather myself and immediately correct him. "It's Vince now. Vince," I say, my lips vibrating against my teeth firmly as I make sure my voice is deeper and stronger than it is in even my most alpha moments. The shock of seeing him has my heart racing, but I'm an expert at covering weak emotions—on the rare occasions that I have them.

I can't believe this guy recognized me?

I spent the decade and a half that I've been away from this area working on the transformation. I put on at least twenty pounds of pure muscle, my beard has grown to a controlled scruff, and daily-wear contacts mean my dark-brown eyes don't hide behind lenses thicker than hickory bacon. Not to mention that every breath I take is a controlled study in hyper-masculinity, from my voice to how I hold my body to my lack of overly expressive emotion. This is Vince. I'm Vince. I'll never be Skinny Vinny again.

"Do I know you?" I ask. He looks exactly the same, maybe even hotter, but I don't want him to think he was ever significant to me. Even though he has had more than an occasional role in my jerk-off fantasies since I was a teenager.

"Come on, it hasn't been that long. It's me, Tack. Tack O'Leary. And, ah, yeah, I'm still Tack," he says. Of course, Tack hasn't had to change a thing about himself since high school including being named after the equipment used on his beloved horses. He was voted Most Popular, Most Athletic and Nicest Eyes. Usually they only let you win in one category but Tack's year was such a landslide they bent the rules. I would have been voted Most Likely to Not be Voted Anything if that was a category since the only people who really knew me were the boys who teased me relentlessly for being a "girly-boy." No one would call me that now.

"Oh, right. I remember now. Your family had a farm," I say, keeping up my charade by pretending to piece the details together in my head and trying not to look at the outline of his dick in his pants. I respect having a great dick or a great ass but having both is really just obnoxious.

"Still do. I've got a load of fresh eggs and some produce under all that hay. I'm taking it to the farmers market in New Hope. But what the hell are you doing in the middle of Route 513 in Pittstown?"

Tack looks me up and down and I can't tell if he is examining my hard-earned muscular body or the fact that I'm dressed for a board meeting, not the side of a country road. I got on the bus right after signing the summer rental agreement with the tenants for my penthouse. I wanted to give them the impression that I was still a powerful master of the universe so they wouldn't balk at the incredibly high monthly charge. They didn't need to know that without the rent money, I would default on the apartment's second mortgage that I'm using to renovate the place in New Hope. A buddy gave me an inside tip about an investment opportunity and I wasn't in a position to be picky about the location.

"I'm actually headed to New Hope," I say, but as soon as the words come out of my mouth I realize I should have given a different answer. Now it sounds like I want a ride, which I do but *not* with him. I'd rather crawl to New Hope on my hands and knees. But first, I would change my pants because they cost more than his beat-up truck.

"Looks like you need a ride," he says. His mouth closes and one side of his smile tightens to show off a sexy grin.

No. There is no way I am getting in that truck with Tack. He is the very last person I wanted to see here. Does Tack know he broke my heart? Does he even remember what he did to me? Inside I'm an almost uncontrollable storm of lust, regret, fear and desire but I take every last feeling and stuff it deep beneath my exterior. Vinny might babble a string of needy requests but Vince knows how to focus and turn the tables.

"Question is," I say, making sure my face remains without expression, "why is Tack O'Leary going to New Hope? Didn't your buddies always say that place was full of queers?"

"Still is," he says without missing a beat. "Some things are still the same but a lot of things aren't." Tack always spoke in riddles. It's just as annoying as ever. "New Hope has the most popular farmers market in all of Bucks County. I'm there helping sell my dad's produce when I have time."

"How is your dad?" I ask just to be polite. Mr. O'Leary was an asshole of major proportions. I'm sure as he has gotten older, he's gotten even more zealous.

"He's the same," Tack says without emotion. "I gotta get going. You in or not?" The tone of Tack's voice either shows he's in a hurry or that asking about his dad hit a raw spot.

"I'll just walk to the general store up ahead and call a

cab. Good luck with your hay, Tack," I say, hoping my tone conveys fuck off.

Tack steps toward me and I can smell the potent mix of sweat and hay on his skin. Reminds me of visits to his farm in high school and waiting for him to finish his chores so we could... I get an immediate semi that I reposition as best I can down the side of my leg so it isn't too obvious.

He walks closer to the truck, stretches his arm in front of me and then opens the passenger side door.

"Get in," he says.

"Like I said, I'm just going to..."

"The general store is closed for renovations and there hasn't been a pay phone there for like ten years." He looks me up and down again. I'm sure he can see my pulsing erection and this time I don't care. Let him see how big it is. Let him see the man I've become. I know he doesn't want to be with me. He made that very clear many years ago. But I don't care. Let him see what he's been missing.

"Get in," he says again, but this time his voice doesn't have any edge.

Against my better judgment, I jump in his vintage pickup truck without saying a word. Once I'm in, he slams the door, and lets that sexy smile linger.

"Next stop, New Hope."

Chapter Two

As soon as we make it over the hill, the expansive countryside opens before me like an antique quilt unfolding at a county fair. Recently mowed fields make perfectly parallel lines that bend with the shape of the land; yellow grassy patches are contained by split rail fences so farm animals can freely graze; newly green trees create small clusters of forest. I never appreciated the beauty of the countryside as a kid.

It would almost feel calm and peaceful if riding in Tack's pickup didn't feel like being put in a cardboard box and kicked across a field. We bump and bounce over every pothole. I'm a few inches taller than Tack and I think he's enjoying making sure my head hits the roof of the cab whenever he can make it happen.

"Do you have to hit every pothole in the road?" I ask.

"It was a rough winter. Roads are still torn up," he says. He glances over at me for a second but I spot a huge ditch ahead.

"Watch out!" I shout with more inflection than I would like. Tack suddenly swerves to avoid the crater and the momentum makes me slide across the bench and right into Tack. For just a second my face brushes against his shoulder. The feel of his body is exhilarating and awkward all at once. I immediately push myself back to the passenger side and fasten my seat belt so it won't happen again. He doesn't say anything but I think I see a smile approach his lips. Tack stares straight ahead; his focus is on the road.

We ride in silence which I am sure surprises him. In high school, I'd blather on about some random poem I loved or a character in a book I was reading. As an adult I learned the power of silence. It can make people uncomfortable and you can use that to your advantage.

I keep my eyes forward without saying a word. I force Tack to make the first move to start a conversation. Let him understand who is in control now. We travel through the countryside and down to the road that hugs the river. It's early summer so the trees are bare enough that I can see the small currents and rapids that punctuate the glassy surface of the Delaware.

"So, you going to New Hope for the weekend or something?" Tack says, caving to the silence.

"Not exactly."

"Well, the radio is broke and we got a slow ten miles until we get there. Maybe you can tell me what the hell you're doing here after, what, more than fifteen years?" I look over at him and I can't tell if he is angry or teasing. Since he's focused on the road I can take a longer look than before. His dirty blond hair has darkened just a bit and his face has filled out so that his chin is even stronger and his jawline even sharper. He looks like he should be on a calendar featuring super-hot farmers.

"So, are you gonna tell me?" he asks.

I snap out of my fantasy and refocus. "Oh, yeah, sure. I mean, I can. No problem." I'm all stumbles and hesitation. That's not Vince, that's Vinny. This guy's got me losing my edge in less than five minutes in his presence. I order myself to pull it together.

"There was an investment opportunity right on the river. Great little inn that fell on hard times. Owners couldn't keep it going so when the deal came across my desk, I realized it had a great ROI." I look at him and jump on this opportunity to show off who I am now. "*That's return on investment*," I say slowly but he doesn't take the bait.

"Got it," he says, staring straight ahead.

Most of what I've told him is true. Not that I'm worried about lying to Tack—he never did place a whole lot of emphasis on telling the truth. I don't tell him that I lost my fortune in a deal that went south after the firm found out I had been fucking one of the biggest investors. I don't tell him my buddy pointed me in the direction of this deal because he knew a hospitality chain was developing a plan to buy a bunch of charming inns and make a conglomerate. I don't tell him how desperate I am to make sure this one shows a profit so that by the end of the summer Fun-

Tyme Inc. will want to add this inn their portfolio and I'll be able to cash out and get back to New York.

I sold off all my toys that had price tags over four figures, rented out my penthouse and decided to come out here just for the summer so I could flip this place, make a huge profit, get back on my feet and go back to New York City.

"And you?" I ask, changing the subject. "What have you been up to?" I don't want to ask it but the next question just falls out of my mouth and I can't stop it. "What happened with you and Evie?" I squeeze my hands into a fist after the question comes out and dig my nails into my hand. Why would I give him even the slightest indication that I care about him and Evie?

"I was wondering when you would ask that," he says. *Oh, screw you, Tack.* I stare straight ahead.

"Just making conversation," I say, throwing the line away, my voice perfectly steady and without a hint of inflection.

"Sure," he says. "Well, about a year or so after high school we got hitched."

"I see." I make sure I show zero emotion on the outside. My insides, though, crash with the pain of knowing, without a doubt, that he never wanted and never could want me. The rejection still smacks me in the heart and makes me feel like a bale of hay he doesn't even know has fallen off his truck.

I look out the window and see the river hug a small, newly green island in the middle of the flow. It's been fifteen years and I'll be here for just the season. What do I care about him and Evie? It doesn't matter how much I

wanted Tack, how often I thought about him or how perfect I thought our lives could be together. It's not what he
wanted. He made that clear; I guess I just never let myself
picture them actually getting married. "I know that's what
you always wanted."

"It was. By the way, which place in New Hope? The
one between the playhouse and the water?" I'm totally
fine with him being the one to change that rancid subject.

"Yeah, The Hideaway Inn. There's a big Memorial Day
weekend luncheon this afternoon in the restaurant."

"The Hideaway? People have been calling that the *Hide-
a-went*. They haven't seen a guest at that place for years.
Restaurant is still open though."

"Thank you, Tack. I am aware."

"Have you seen it recently, though?"

"No. Closed-bid auction. All online. Sight unseen."

"Oh…" His eyes widen like I just said I purchased an
ancient ruin.

"What's that supposed to mean?"

"Ah, nothing." There is a slight but noticeable mocking
laugh in his voice.

"Look, stop being an asshole," I say.

"Asshole? I'm the one who picked you up off the side
of the road."

"Yeah, well, you are also the one who…" I'm about to
bring up the past when I see a sign on the road that reads
"New Hope, this way." Tack takes the turn. "Never mind,"
I say and we go back to a chilly silence.

We cross over from New Jersey to Pennsylvania on the
New Hope-Lambertville Bridge. New Hope looks like

something out of a Norman Rockwell painting—small, boldly painted colonial-style buildings line a river walk with trees, fountains and a gazebo. The historic Bucks County Playhouse that was once a gristmill proudly anchors the landscape.

As we turn on to Main Street I realize that the town is more like a Norman Rockwell painting if old Norm had been a power-bottom with a social activist consciousness. Rainbow flags hang from almost every storefront, same-sex couples walk hand in hand and "Love is love" signs cover the town like it's a mandatory municipal ordinance.

"Never any place to park in this town. Okay to use the parking at the Hide-a-went?" Tack asks.

"Sure," I say. "But if you call it that again I'll make sure you're towed into the Delaware." I'm kidding, of course, I wouldn't have his truck towed into the river. I'd just push it in myself.

Tack pulls in front of The Hideaway Inn and I see my investment for the first time. A three-story stately stone home that, according to my research, was built in the mid-eighteenth century by a wealthy farmer who wanted to have a place on the river away from his crops. I imagine he also had some side-action in town. There are more windows than a typical structure from the time period, and the previous owner blew out the back of the place so that the dining area and guest rooms have huge, expansive windows and a sundeck with amazing views of the river.

Once Tack pulls into the tiny lot I grab my bag and get out of the truck. "I won't be parked long, just need to drop these vegetables and eggs off at the Ferry Market on the next block," he says. "See you around."

"Sure," I say and watch him walk away carrying a crate of produce that make his triceps flex so hard they look like sleek torpedoes ready to be fired. No. I will not spend the summer lusting after Tack. Again. I'll make sure I don't see Tack again while I'm in New Hope. I'll avoid him with the same enthusiasm I avoid porta potties at outdoor music festivals. If I do run into him on the street I'll simply run into oncoming traffic or set myself on fire. My latest, and currently sole, investment is right in front of me. Time to start understanding what I've gotten myself into.

On closer inspection of the inn, I notice a few details that I need to take care of: painting the peeling trim with a brighter color, fixing the blue shutters that cling to the edges of the windows like their lives depend on it, and getting rid of those garish pride flags that make the place look cluttered. I look up to the third floor where the owner's suite is located and make a mental note to replant the window boxes with red geraniums before the weeds reach past the windows.

I look at my watch and realize I only have about forty minutes until the LGBTQ Historical Society arrives for their annual Memorial Day Weekend luncheon. While the guest rooms have been closed for some time, the cafe has been running continuously thanks to the dedication of the restaurant manager, Anita Patel, who I have been phoning and emailing with since the sale. She impressed me with her no-nonsense attitude even if she thinks I work for her rather than the other way around. She thought this luncheon would be a good way to introduce the new ownership and get to know the most powerful LGBTQ community members. I just wanted to know how much we were charging and the bottom-line profit for the event. Anita avoided a real answer but mentioned a "community discount" for the group, which I honored, but that won't be happening again. It's a business, not a charity.

I open the front door to the cafe. Ruffled burgundy curtains that look like they were put up the night disco was invented sag over the windows and shabby white napkins sit sadly on threadbare tablecloths. Some of the walls are painted a cheery yellow. Others have wallpaper from what must have been an ancient asylum for the criminally ugly and still others are painted bright blue. It's the opposite of my favorite places in New York, all of which have dark colors and stark exposed steel beams. Still, there is a part deep inside me that finds this place cozy and warm. There is even a crackling fire in the massive brick fireplace that covers the entire back wall and it helps take off the late-May chill. The place definitely needs a good deal of work but that's what I'm here to do.

BOOM!

A small hydrogen bomb has exploded. I walk toward the sound and swing open the door to the kitchen. A woman in chef's gear and an older, slightly frail man wearing a waiter's uniform are standing a few inches from each other, arguing. The floor is covered with cookware, trays and what look like raw Cornish game hens.

"What the fuck?" I shout as I barge through the doors.

"I cannot work with this imbecile anymore. He ruined the entire meal," the woman in the chef's uniform barks at me. "We have nothing to serve to half the guests!" Carla. The chef. Anita had described her as small but tightly wound.

"You weren't paying attention *as usual* and knocked over the tray. I wasn't even on that side of the kitchen, dearie," the man says, his tone as pointed as a needle. He must be Clayton the waiter.

"Where's Anita?" I demand, looking at the clock above the back door and realizing we don't have much time until the luncheon.

"Who are you?" Carla asks in full attack mode.

"I'm Vince," I shoot back at her. "The new owner."

"Great. The first thing you can do is fire him. Now!" Chef Carla points at Clayton, who gives me a look like someone ran over his cat.

"I have been at this cafe over twenty years. How dare you," he says.

"How dare I? I'm the chef," Carla retorts.

"Let's all stay calm," I say, despite the fact that it feels like things are already out of control. "We have some important guests arriving very soon. Let's work this out *after* we have a successful lunch."

More general screaming between the two erupts.

Oh, hell no. "Stop it!" I finally shout louder than both of them. They shut up immediately.

Chef Carla points her finger at me. "I do not want that man in my kitchen one second longer. Fire him. Now!"

I do not do well with people telling me what to do. At. All. "We will work this out *after* lunch, *I said*."

There is a moment of silence and then Carla unties her apron and throws it on the ground.

Oh no.

"I have worked in kitchens up and down the river and I refuse to have my authority undermined. I am the chef. What I say is law. Maybe you don't understand how a kitchen works."

She couldn't be more right but I'm not about to let her know that.

"I quit!" she shouts and walks out the door.

Normally if someone under me threw a tantrum like that I would hold the door open for them as they walked out, but with guests about to arrive, I need her. The last meal I cooked involved a microwave and soggy leftover pizza.

I walk out the back door of the kitchen and run after her. "Carla, wait!" I say but she quickly barrels down Main Street. "Carla!" I yell but she is too far away or pretending not to hear me. Either way, I'm screwed. I yell out, "Carla! Carla!" like I am looking for a lost dog. A few people stare at me and I don't think it can get much worse until something rolls over my left foot.

Chapter Three

"Ow!" I shout.

"Why the hell did I see our chef walking away from the restaurant when the luncheon is about to begin?"

"Hey, roll off my foot," I plead.

"When you tell me what happened to our chef."

"*Our* chef?" I ask the crazy woman in a wheelchair.

"Duh, yes. I'm obviously Anita. We've been emailing for weeks. How many butch Indian women using wheelchairs do you think there are in this small town?" she asks, using her hand control to maneuver her chair enough to release the pressure on my foot. "And obviously, you're Vince."

Anita does not wait for confirmation. She rolls into high gear and tourists are forced to jump off the curb out of her way. She seems like she couldn't care less as her long silk scarf flows behind her. I jog to keep up.

"Wait!" I say, and she finally slows her roll when we get to the tiny parking lot.

"We don't have time. We have to find someone to finish the meal." She does a pivot turn right in front of Tack's truck.

"Don't you have a backup cook?" I ask her, assuming she must know someone.

"No, I do not have a backup cook!" I have obviously pissed her off. "You think I also keep a pocket Chef Boyardee in the back of my wheelchair or have Rachael Ray in my phone contacts?"

"I'm sorry. I'm desperate here." I do not want to have to use one of my least favorite words in the English language—*refund*. I'm angry at myself for not getting here earlier but I had the closing in New York and the last of my things to pack. The frustration builds and I punch the first thing in front of me, which just happens to be Tack's truck.

"Don't hurt Axel, he didn't do nothing to you except get your ass to town." Tack pets the rearview mirror of the truck like it's a rescued kitten.

Where the hell did Tack come from? I'm in the middle of an emergency that I'm sure can't be solved by a sexy farm boy. "Don't you have some radishes to peddle?" I ask, dismissing him.

"My cousin Richard is, as you say, peddling today. I just made the delivery," he says, ignoring my tone and responding with a more playful one.

"Tack, you're here. I'm so glad. We need your help,"

Anita says. Suddenly her scowl turns to sweet roses talking to Tack. He may know how to charm Anita but my association with Tack ended when I got out of his truck.

"What happened?" Tack asks me. "You've only been here ten minutes."

"Yeah, and in that time the chef quit and half the food for lunch has been destroyed. Tack, do you think you can help us?" Anita asks.

"Let me see," he says, and walks to the blue-painted door set in the old stone wall at the back of the inn.

I'm about to throw myself in front of the door like the inn has been quarantined but Tack is inside before I have a chance. "What makes you think some redneck farm boy knows anything about cooking?" I ask Anita, assuming Tack will be useless to help.

"He just finished his first year at Bucks Culinary. I think he knows more than either of us," she says and wheels through the back door.

Tack? Culinary school? The guy who spent most of his time with crops and horses is training to be a chef? They guy who survived the summer on beefy jerky, Mountain Dew and leftover Easter jelly beans? I'll believe it when I see it. I follow them both to the kitchen.

"Hey, Clayton," Tack says as he walks inside.

"Oh, Tack, I'm so grateful you're here. That witch has lost her mind. I wasn't anywhere near the hens. She must have knocked them over. Not me," Clayton says. His voice is high-pitched and he has a slight lisp. He is exactly the kind of guy Tack's buddies would have made fun of on one of their trips to New Hope. But Clayton seems to know Tack; he even takes comfort in the fact that Tack is here.

Tack looks around the kitchen, takes a quick inventory of the walk-in fridge, grabs some things from the pantry and turns on the oven.

"What do you think?" Anita asks.

Tack walks past Anita and Clayton and stands in front of me. "I think I'm going to save your ass for the second time today," he says with a sly smile. He's enjoying this. His face is right next to mine. I can almost feel his breath on my skin. I make sure my eyes are cold and blank despite feeling hot and excited. I make sure no emotion escapes.

"I'll be right back," Tack says and heads out the door. I'm able to finally release the air I've been tightly holding in my lungs.

"Wait a minute. Do you two know each other?" Anita asks.

"Oh, dearie, isn't it obvious?" Clayton adds.

"No," I say. "We do not know each other. I mean, we used to. I mean, we went to the same school, that's all."

Clayton looks me up and down. "Just like I said. They know each other." He makes the word *know* sound dirty.

"Anita, I do not want Tack anywhere near this place let alone cooking lunch. I want him out!"

"Oh, sure," she says, smiling like a crocodile. "We'll just throw away the food, refund everyone's money. Is that what you want to do?"

She knows full well what a last-minute cancellation would do to our goodwill with the community.

"Fine." I realize I have no other options, but I hate the

fact that Tack is swooping in—for the second time today—to save my (very firm) ass. I am not here to rely on anyone, and certainly not Tack O'Leary.

"Luckily," Tack says, kicking the door open with his foot, "we didn't need all of this at the farm stand." He's carrying a box of bright green and dark reddish-purple lettuce with some radishes and carrots poking out. The way he is holding the box makes his biceps form perfect peaks on each side. I'm about to lose the last investment I have and I'm fantasizing about this guy's biceps. *Focus, Vince.* Work and sex do not mix. Anymore.

"Look, I can't just take your stuff," I say.

"You're not. I'm going to invoice you for this. This is prime local, organic produce. It doesn't grow on trees," he says. "I mean, the cherries and apricots do but you know what I mean." He gives me that grin, that cocky grin I know better than any grin. But this time I am forty percent sure he's flirting with me. Maybe forty-two percent.

"Here is what we are going to do," he says. "I have some strawberries on my truck and saw club soda in the fridge. Clayton, you make pitchers of spritzers with a few good bottles of chardonnay from the wine storage and what I saw in the fridge. Vinny…"

My entire body tenses when I hear that name and he can tell.

"Sorry, Vince," he says calmly. He gently hands me a pair of scissors. "You use these scissors to cut the Cornish game hens in half that didn't mop the floor. That way we'll have enough for each person and they'll cook a lot faster. I'll use the greens and whatever else I can find to make a nice salad and a side. Anita, you be your charming self and greet the guests and help Clayton with the drinks. By the time Clayton has them full of wine, all of this will be ready."

Clayton and Anita hop to their jobs but I'm immobile. Tack O'Leary is in the kitchen of my inn preparing lunch for the New Hope LGBTQ Historical Society. I watch him take off his flannel shirt to reveal his golden body already freckled for the summer. He extends his arm to grab one of the aprons hanging near the walk-in fridge and his biceps and triceps lengthen, showing off the smooth curves and sinewy muscles of his arms. He ties the apron on behind his back and an entirely different set of muscles are on display.

"Vince, those scissors, right there. Cut each one from here to here," he says, pointing at the tiny chickens. At first, I bristle at being told what to do, but one glance at the clock tells me I don't have time to be a hard-ass if I want this luncheon to not be a disaster.

I quickly start working on my task. I try to focus on what I'm doing so I don't wind up serving a side of my thumb with the dish, but it's hard to do that and keep sneaking glances at Tack, not to mention my hands are covered in slimy chicken guts. I notice that Tack didn't assign me the cocktail or salad task.

I also notice the way he moves around the kitchen is masterful. It's not just his confidence, it's seeing him do something he seems to truly love. It reminds me of watching him during football games. He was mesmerizing on the field, like a Greek god in tight pants. I'd sit in the bleachers with the marching band as assholes threw crumpled-up pieces of paper with witty expressions like "Skinny Vinny is a fag." I was so focused on watching Tack play that I barely noticed until I had to clean out my tuba. I think I filled an entire notebook of erotic poetry about him in that uniform.

I finish my first and hopefully last stint as a country butcher and shake all of the pornographic images of Tack from my mind. It's time to turn on the charm with my first guests. I freshen up in the bathroom by wiping the mud off my shoes and retying my tie. I splash some water on my face and smooth my thick black hair down so my appearance is polished and professional. I look at myself in the mirror for a second and think about my band uniform and that dumb tuba. No one would ever have thought that skinny, shy kid with acne would turn into a square-jawed, thickly muscled alpha with a perfect smile and flawless skin. Well, my orthodontist, dermatologist and personal trainer would, of course, but my secrets are safe with them.

Anita wheels ahead of me and I follow her into the dining room, and it's filled with about twenty people. The last time I spoke in front of a group this size was the board at the firm—a room with windows larger than the entire inn overlooking Wall Street, one enormous glossy table, and about two dozen elderly white men all wearing dark suits and sour expressions.

I feel like I have walked through some kind of inversion portal.

Sitting at small tables under the exposed wooden beams holding up the low ceiling is the most diverse group of people I may have ever seen in one room. There are women, men and all gender expressions in between and beyond that range. Some look much younger than me while others are

1

clearly past retirement age. I wouldn't guess at the ethnicity of anyone but it's clear this group represents a wide range.

"Everyone," Anita says, clinking a spoon to a water glass. "I am pleased to introduce you to Vincent Amato, the new owner of The Hideaway Inn." Everyone politely applauds.

I nod and smile. "Thank you. Please call me Vince," I say. "I'm thrilled to be here and excited about the upcoming changes."

"What do you mean 'upcoming changes'?" a person dressed in a violet dress over men's suit pants and wearing a vintage emerald and black lace hat asks as she uses one hand to quiet the rest of the group.

"Vince," Anita says, stepping in. "This is Serilda Jackson. *They* are the president of the LGBTQ Historical Society." Anita emphasizes the word *they* as if I've been living in a corporate boardroom for the last decade but I'm more than aware of what it feels like to be named and misnamed.

"My pronouns are they, them, theirs. I can't make it any clearer and anyone who messes them up makes a voluntary ten-dollar donation to the society on the spot." Serilda's voice is pure Southern fried honey and hot sauce. They extend their hand to me and smile deliberately. I'm not sure if I should kiss or grip it firmly but I choose a light shake. "Now, what do you mean by upcoming changes?" they repeat.

"Well, to be honest…" I start and immediately stop myself. Nothing can kill a business faster than rumors of a corporate takeover. If I tell them—or anyone—my plan to sell to a national chain, I can pretty much count on the customer base shrinking. Not to mention some angry on-line reviews. I quickly shut my mouth.

"This town has always had a strong connection to our community. Our expectation is that the businesses in New Hope will honor that relationship. What do you plan to do? We don't want some corporate chain coming in here and changing the local character," Serilda presses.

This person is no joke. I have met some real sharks on Wall Street but Serilda could hold their own with any titan of industry. I have no intention of telling them that FunTyme Inc. couldn't care less who dines at the Inn once they buy it as long as the tables keep turning. All money is green. I also don't tell them that I didn't go to a single meeting of the LGBTQ group in college or that I always schedule work out of town during the Pride Parade. I *also* don't tell them that I annually donate buckets of money to the LGBTQ No Name Calling Week national orga-nizing committee. That detail is just between me and my accountant.

"Mr. Amato. What do you plan to do?" they repeat.

"Well…"

The door to the kitchen opens and Tack appears. His radiant smile and energy cut through the tension. "Wel-come, everyone. Lunch is served," he says, and Clayton begins placing plates of perfectly roasted chicken and fresh salad at the tables.

Serilda walks over to me but now their smile is friendly and gentle. "Why didn't you tell me you hired Tack? Oh, he's a fine young man. Now I know you have your priorities right." Serilda squeezes my arm gently and goes to sit at their table.

I look back at the kitchen door and see that Tack has been watching me. He isn't beaming that searchlight smile anymore. Instead he has a smaller, more intense smile that he is throwing directly at me and me alone.

I've been out of New York City less than a day and Tack has already saved me more than once. Maybe he thinks this somehow makes up for lost time or evens the score from when we were kids.

Nice try, Tack, but you aren't running the show anymore. I am.

Chapter Four

I wait until the minted fruit cups are served and tea service has begun before I walk back into the kitchen. Tack is wiping down the steel counters. I avoid eye contact as I walk past him behind the line and go right to my bag to get my checkbook.

"What did they say?" Tack asks anxiously. "Are people enjoying everything? Was there enough seasoning on the hen? Too much garlic in the dressing? I know some people don't like garlic at lunch but the greens were a bit bitter so I wanted…"

Shock number three thousand for the day. Tack isn't cocky about his talent? The lunch was fantastic. The truth is everyone in the dining room was raving about the meal. I assumed Tack knew it was excellent but hearing him ask all these questions tells me how he really feels. He's insecure. He's nervous and anxious about what people are saying about him—and I love it. After everything he did to me all those years ago, part of me can't help wanting to see him knocked down a few pegs. He deserves it.

"Oh, the food? Is that what you are asking about? Yeah," I say, "I think it was fine. No one complained." I open my checkbook without looking at him. "Invoice me for the produce but I want to pay you right now for your time. Just tell me your day rate. I'll beat it by twenty percent because this was a rush. That's standard."

Tack comes out from behind the line and takes off his apron. I refuse to look over at him. This is how our story ends. This is how I say goodbye to Tack—on my terms with a big fat check that says *Fuck you* in the memo line. Well, I might leave that out because I don't need the bank knowing how petty I am, but I will trace the words in the memo without leaving a mark.

"Zero. I don't have a rate," he says.

"Well, let me ask Anita when she comes in what the local rate is and we can use that. Plus the twenty percent I already mentioned."

"No, I mean, I don't want to get paid for cooking today. I was just helping you out." He balls up his apron and throws it in the hamper. He walks closer to me.

"No," I say. "That's not possible. You work. You get paid. That's how business operates. Now why don't I just say five hundred?" I sit down at the small desk by the door and turn to a blank check.

"No," he says.

"I respect good negotiators. Fine," I say. "Let's do seven-fifty." I do not look up from the checkbook or get up from the desk. I stay calm, focused and cold. He thinks he can make up for everything that went down between us in high school by throwing a few hens in the oven and tossing a salad. I don't think so.

"No, Vince," Tack says. His voice is firm and strong but not angry. His natural strength feels like the real deal unlike the show I'm putting on. I hear him taking a few steps closer until I can feel him standing directly behind me. I can hear his breathing and feel the heat from his body against my back.

"You don't understand," he says, and puts his right hand gently on my shoulder. Feeling him reach for me and having him intentionally touch me sends a rush of excitement throughout my body but I am able to kill it quickly. I turn any feelings of desire I might have to anger and frustration. It's the way I have learned to protect myself and it always works.

"What?" I snap at him, flinching away from him and turning in the chair. "What don't I understand? Please tell me. Tell me what someone with an Ivy League MBA doesn't understand about business that a farm boy from rural nowhere does. Please, enlighten me with your business acumen, or are the words I'm using too big for you?"

Tack has never seen this side of me—the pissed-off alpha male who more than once has made someone who works under him cry. I'm not sure if he's confused, pissed or hurt, and I don't care. I write a check for one thousand dollars, stand up and shove it in his hand. There. Take that, Tack.

He looks at me and then down at the ridiculous amount of money I'm flashing at him. He holds the check in my face, rips it in half and says, "Fuck," and then rips it in half the other way and says, "you." The pieces float to the floor and he walks out the door.

I tell myself I couldn't be happier and it almost doesn't even feel like a lie.

Chapter Five

Tack

I'm not taking Vinny's money. I'm not taking anything from him. Who does he think he is throwing money at me like that? More importantly who is this guy who vaguely resembles Vinny but acts like Darth Vader and sounds like Barry White before he's had his coffee?

Damn, this kid always knew how to press my buttons. But he isn't a kid anymore. He's definitely become a man. The way he struts around in that expensive suit like he came back owning the place, which I guess he did since he is the owner of the Hide-a-went, but he doesn't need all that attitude.

I sit in my truck and think about getting out, walking

into the kitchen and telling Vinny to cut the crap. I'll tell
him to get back in the truck and me and him will just drive
around the rolling countryside until we run out of gas, and
then we'll put a blanket down and fall asleep under the stars.

I slam my hands against the wheel of my truck. "Damn!"
As soon as I realize what I've done, I apologize. "Sorry,
Axel. You know how this guy makes me crazy," I tell my
truck. I turn the key in the ignition and the motor starts
chugging. The familiar sputters and spurts calm me down.
We head back over the bridge to New Jersey. Since this
luncheon put a serious delay in my day, I'll barely have time
to make it back to the farm and then back over to Pennsylvania for the last week of the spring semester at school. At
least I'll only have one class in the summer session. Right
now, I'm constantly backtracking from the farm to New
Hope to school to New Hope. Poor Axel barely knows
which way he's going some days but it's the only way to
get off the farm and into the kitchen. It's not just the physical miles that take a toll on me, it's navigating the different
worlds. The farm may only be a dozen miles from the rainbow flags, drag bars and community pride parades of New
Hope but once I cross the river I'm in a different world.

I convince myself that cutting across on Grafton Hollow will make the trip quicker. I know it won't and I don't
really have time to go out of my way, but still I can't help
myself from driving by Vinny's old house. The old road
snakes along a seasonal stream but eventually leads me right
to the spot I've been avoiding for years. His square house
sits alone on a small patch of land with woods in the back
and fields on the three other sides.

The faded red split-level looks as bad as it did the day I first met Vinny—broken gutters, peeling paint and the same cracked window in the door. That day, I was fixing the fence way back at the far end of our farm. School had ended a few weeks back and my dad gave me the summer to get the fence in shape before needing me in the fields. We had more acreage back then and the farm felt like a kingdom that expanded off the page of the map. I'd walk to the edge of the farm each morning to work on a new section of fence and feel like I was on the brink of something about to happen.

I was struggling to hammer a brace into a post at a section where the fence ran against the property line of Vinny's house. I'd always thought the house had been abandoned years before but I saw this kid in black jeans and black T-shirt come out carrying a book.

"Hey!" I yelled out. "Can you hold this brace for me? Will only take a second." The kid kept walking but I knew he heard me so I got up and yelled louder. "It will only take a second. We're neighbors. Come on."

He stood there without moving, like an animal trying to be invisible in front of his prey.

"Pleeeaaaassse!" I squealed in a funny high-pitched voice like I was stuck in a cartoon desert and he had a bucket of water. I watched him soften just a bit. He looked up just enough for me to see that the corners of his mouth were fighting a smile. Then he walked over.

"Thanks, man, I'm Tack."

"Vinny," he said but nothing else. His eyes stayed down.

"You go to Eisenhower High?" I asked since I hadn't

seen him before and a kid like this would definitely stand out at school. He had dark piercing eyes that were delicate yet distant. His hair was even darker and the bangs that fell down one side of his face were dyed the color of eggplants during harvest.

"Starting this year." The words came out of his mouth like each one was a struggle.

"The teachers are a pain in the ass but the coaches are okay. You play any sports?"

"I do not," he said and I could see his eyes roll back and his shoulders hunch toward his ears.

"Can you just hold this brace right here while I hammer?"

Vinny used his free hand to hold the brace but he wasn't strong enough to hold it in place with just one arm.

"Can you put down the book and use both hands?" I asked.

"Put the book down? Where?" he asked, looking around as if he was expecting a bookcase to magically reveal itself on the edge of the field.

"Just on the ground," I said, wondering what exactly I had gotten myself into.

"Are you out of your mind? This is Chekhov. I won't just throw it on the ground," he said defiantly. His stubbornness was never something he could control.

"It's just a book and it's summer anyway. You ain't gotta read."

"I don't have to read this book. I *want* to. It's a play about these sisters and they live in this small town in Russia and they are totally bored and the people in the town don't get them *at all* so they make this plan to move to the big city. I haven't finished it yet but I can't wait until they get to Moscow."

When he spoke about the book his entire demeanor changed. He didn't seem shy or scared of anything. His eyes opened wide and he gestured wildly with his hands and arms. It was like someone had just changed his batteries. He talked about the worlds he was reading in a way that made me as excited as him. No one I hung out with read over the summer or talked about some sisters moving to Moscow or worried about putting a book on the dirt. Who was this kid? He seemed strange and familiar all at once to me.

"Hold on, I've got an idea." He put his book under one arm and grabbed the brace with both hands so I could hammer it in easily. He had more strength in his body than I had assumed.

That summer Vinny would come by and see me almost every day, usually with a new book. I loved hearing him talk. He described the spiritual journey of Siddhartha, the complicated plot of King Lear and even read some of James Baldwin's poems to me that were so riveting I almost hammered my finger to a post. At school I was in a class called "Reading Foundations" and even I was smart enough to know it was for kids who were barely passing. I never felt dumb around Vinny. He treated me like I was just as smart as he was and after hanging out with him for a few weeks, I started to believe it.

Being alone with Vinny was easy. We were so different but also had so much in common. My mom died when I was a kid and he never knew his father. I never talked to anyone about not really having many memories of her and wanting more. He only had a single picture of his dad and never wanted to know more. We fit like opposite pieces of a puzzle that click when joined. Being alone together at the edge of the farm felt like freedom. But when the fence was done and school started, the world shifted back to where it was and whatever we had evaporated.

A small-town high school is a network of territories with strict borders. Vinny didn't belong anywhere and it made his life miserable but it made me admire him more because he didn't need to. He did what he wanted, how he wanted to do it.

My life felt like an endless list of obligations. I followed some script then and I don't even know why or where it came from. I had to place at the meets, have the hottest girlfriend, drink like an animal at parties on the weekends. These things were expected of me or I expected them of myself. At the time I couldn't tell the difference. I couldn't imagine a life being anything other than the one that was already attached to me, but meeting Vinny put a crack in that heavy iron chain.

Once school started, Evie came back from her summer job down the shore, football practice began and chores on the farm took over my life. At least, that's what I told myself. I couldn't find a way to make Vinny part of my life beyond that summer without making my entire world explode. I ignored him at school, pretty much, even though alone in bed at night I couldn't stop thinking about him. I kept those worlds separate because they seemed to be in completely different orbits. It was a shitty thing to do. I know it now and I even knew it then.

I left The Hideaway mad as hell at Vinny—or rather *Vince*—for the way he treated me in the kitchen, but the truth is I deserve everything he said to me and more. How could I ever get him to understand the choices I made back then and why I made them? How could I explain to him how hard I have worked to undo everything I did back then? Then I remember how I already started on the wrong foot. He asked about Evie and I went all mysterious and vague. I should have told him we got divorced. I should have told him that we still co-parent a wonderful, funny six-year-old. I should definitely have told him that I finally came out as bi. But picking him up on the side of the road was such a confusing surprise that my brain wasn't functioning at full capacity.

A car flies past me with a series of aggressive honks and I'm back to reality. "Crap, Axel, we gotta blaze," I tell my truck after I catch a glimpse of the clock on the dashboard. We kick into gear and pull up to the farm much later than I usually do. My father is standing on the porch that wraps around the white farmhouse, propping himself up with his cane.

"Where have you been?" he asks.

"Dad, you shouldn't be out on the porch, it's too cold out still. Did the nurse say it was okay to be out like this?" I ask as I grab the crates from the farmers market and start putting them in the storage barn near the house.

"I don't take orders from her or anyone."

As soon as my back is turned I roll my eyes. My dad has

slowed down over the past couple of years almost to the point of being immobile, but while his body has weakened his ornery personality has not.

"Where have you been?" he barks at me again. I'm thirty-five but he treats me like I'm still fifteen. I guess the fact that I moved back into the farmhouse after the divorce didn't help me mature any in his eyes. Divorce is a sin right up there with other sins of the flesh but living here is the only way I can pay for classes at culinary school. Everything in New Hope is too expensive but I keep looking hoping I can find a deal like the one Evie got.

I need to just drop off the materials and crates and get on the road to school. I can't be late today. We have a special event with a chef visiting from a restaurant in Philly. He's doing a demo of some pan-to-plate sauces and I've been looking forward to seeing his technique for weeks. I know I can grasp it if I just watch an expert do it in front of me. This kind of event only happens once a semester.

"Sorry I'm so late," I say, staying focused on moving the crates. "They're working on the bridge over on Headquarters Road." It's true they are working on the bridge. I didn't drive that way but still I'm not technically lying. My God understands. His? Maybe not so much.

"Dad, you should sit down. Your legs are still getting their strength back after your flu."

He hears me but stays leaning on his cane on the porch.

"How were sales at the market today? Is your cousin Richard having any problems?"

"He seems fine but really, Dad, I've got this..." Before I can finish I see him tremble.

"Dad!" I say, running up to the porch, but his legs have started to give way and he begins to fall. I leap up the steps and grab him in my arms just before his body tumbles over. I drag him over to the rocker. The sudden imbalance has clearly startled him. His eyes seem hollow and his complexion is gray.

"Are you okay, Dad?" He doesn't respond but then almost nods. This is as close as he would ever come to admitting he needs help. "I'll get you some water and then I'll call the nurse so she can give you a once-over."

"She's in...will take her over an hour to get here..." He seems stable but is clearly out of breath. He's not in immediate danger but I know he is rattled. I can't leave here until the nurse arrives and checks him out. He may be the most difficult person anyone has ever met but he's still my dad.

"Don't worry, Dad." I pull open the screen door to the kitchen to fetch his water but pause in the doorway. "I can skip school. Nothing important going on today anyway."

Chapter Six

The door to the kitchen swings open and Anita rolls in. "Where's Tack?"

"I don't know," I say, putting my checkbook back in my bag. My plan is to never see him again.

"Well, you better find out. Catered events are one thing but a full dinner service is another. We need a chef."

"I know that." The fact is, we need to get dinner service started as soon as possible before this place goes so deep in the red it looks like a GOP stronghold. My buddy Barry at FunTyme confided in me that they want to start looking at properties and doing closings soon so I have to move quickly if I want a chance at making this place an attractive enough prospect for the investors. I should be thinking about how I'm going to move the needle on the books for this place, but I can't seem to get Tack off my mind.

If I had thought for a second that buying this place would mean I would lay eyes on Tack again I would have opened an Etsy store and sold yarn art or kitten bobbleheads or whatever crap people sell online. Anything to avoid Tack and the mess of emotions that go so well with him, like his ridiculously tight jeans. Can he seriously work in those? The image of his perfect ass from this morning races across my mind and I kick it out.

At least I showed him. Showed him that I'm not so easily manipulated anymore, that I'm in charge, that I've become the man no one ever thought I would be. At least, I think I showed him that. He must have noticed I've changed. Or did he show me, tearing up that check like some diva?

"Tack has culinary school on the other side of Doylestown. He has to pass through New Hope on his way back to school after the farm. I'll call him and see if he can meet with us tonight." Anita takes her cell phone out from a pouch on the side of her chair.

"No!" I don't want to yell at her but I do not want her to make that call. "Look," I say, softening. "It's been a long day and I know you have been phenomenal keeping this place going. I just want to unpack and take a minute to get my bearings. Let's you and I meet tomorrow morning. We don't need to talk to Tack tonight—or at any point. There is no way he can work here."

"But he has totally proven he has the skills."

"It's not about skills. It's about history. I know his wife, Evie. There is no way she is ever going to let her husband take a job at an inn that I own. It will never happen. I can promise you that."

I can still see Evie's face when she cornered me outside the back door of the band rehearsal room. "He doesn't want anything to do with you. You got that? Stay away from him." She adjusted her bra so that her breasts were at attention, sneered at me one more time, and went back to twirling her baton.

"I'm going upstairs to unpack," I tell Anita, grab my bag and head toward the stairs at the back of the kitchen. I want to take off my suit and review every stupid decision I've made in the past few months, from buying this inn to forgetting to download more *Law & Order* reruns.

"Look, Vince. You may know history but it's ancient history."

I stop with my foot on the first step. "What's that supposed to mean?"

"Tack and Evie got divorced," Anita says and rolls toward the kitchen door.

"Excuse me? The Prom Queen and King have called it quits?"

"I'm not a gossip. It's not my story to tell but you got your facts wrong. Evie is not an issue. She's changed. And they are not together in that way anymore." Anita leaves and I head up the stairs toward the owner's suite.

Why didn't Tack tell me he and Evie got divorced? I think back to our conversation in his truck and I realize he didn't say they were still married. He only told me they got married. I think about the ride, and the sun coming in through the driver's side window that made the light hair on his forearms glow over his newly tanned arms. I can see the curve of his pectoral muscle just under his open shirt and how the breeze teased me by blowing it back and forth, revealing and concealing his perfect body.

I walk up the last few stairs, open the door to my new place and strip down to my boxers. I'm too tired to even look around my temporary home. I make it past all the boxes to the bed and collapse on top of it.

Chapter Seven

I wake up two hours later with a raging hard-on, not just typical morning wood but full-on dick of steel that could hammer nails into two-by-fours for the rest of the afternoon. I haven't had an erection like this since I was a teenager and…

My muscles tense and I try not to finish the thought but it relentlessly pulses through me. High school. Watching Tack at the farm and praying his father doesn't find me. The excitement and fear combined like atoms in a molecule. I think about Tack's sweaty body stacking bales of hay from the barn as I watch through a knot in the old barn wood. He tosses each mammoth bale with so much force I expect it to launch into space. My weak arms couldn't even budge one of them but Tack has few obstacles. He's in sync with the world and it's his confidence and ease that made me so turned on then, and being around him again is clearly the reason I now have one hand grabbing my cock and another one squeezing my nipple.

I spit on my palm so I can rub my hand over the head of my dick with more friction. I let my hands enjoy the impact of my last kettle bell workout as they move across my chest. I was so stressed by the move that the workout was even more strenuous than usual and muscles are still sore so that means enough tissue broke in order to repair, stronger, thicker and tougher. That's what change is. You need to break things to make things happen.

It's humid in the apartment without any of the windows open so there is some sweat in the hairy valley between my pecs. I grab my dick and jerk off quickly, my hand bouncing on my shaft and hitting me in the abdomen. A fantasy tries to creep across my brain but I don't let it. I focus on myself, my shaft and the pleasure I am giving myself. This load is about me and giving myself the release I want. The release I need. It only takes a few beats to get me where I need to be.

Then I remember exactly why I'm so horny. I shoot my load thinking it will release all thoughts of him with it but even after my climax I can't stop thinking about Tack.

I wish I could say I don't remember the last time I saw him but that memory has never let go of me.

I was going through a serious James Baldwin phase senior year of high school. Even though I had moved on to reading the poems he wrote while in Paris, I came across a used copy of *The Fire Next Time* at the bookstore. I had read it a few months earlier and Baldwin's description of transforming racial prejudice and hate with love captivated my foolishly idealistic mind. Tack had been ignoring me at school and I thought if I could just do something to remind him of the time we spent together over the summer he would open up to me again and we could pick up where we left off. I bought the book for Tack and planned to find a way to give it to him before school ended.

I could have left it at the farm but his dad scared the crap out of me.

In my stupid, naïve head I thought there was something romantic about leaving the book at school for him, a step toward making our very private relationship public.

I remember being scared and excited the day I brought the book to school. He had math after my calc class and while everyone was in the hall changing classes, I carefully slipped a note on his chair without anyone seeing. My hands trembled as I tossed the paper down. I wrote that I would leave something for him on the tables behind the school under the pine trees. No one ever used those tables so I knew he wouldn't have any problem finding the gift.

After school I hid behind one of the trees and waited for Tack to pick up the book. I couldn't wait to see his beautiful face unwrap the package and start reading. It felt like hours until I finally saw him come out of the building.

As soon as he got close to the tables, his eyes darted over to the book. He was alone. My heart went into my throat. We weren't at my house or at the farm. This was happening at school, in the world.

But then Evie appeared. She ran over to him and wrapped

her arms around him like she always did, treating him more like a prize than a human. Maybe she saw me behind the tree or maybe she didn't but she pulled Tack toward her and gave him a sloppy kiss. She grabbed his hand and led him down the sidewalk away from school.

I stood behind the tree for a while, hoping Tack would return, but he didn't. It started to rain and instead of grabbing the book I just let it sit there. I had always thought of books as sacred objects that needed to be preserved at all costs but maybe they weren't worth protecting at all. Maybe protection wasn't something someone provided for you. Maybe you had to learn to do it yourself.

The clouds turned darker. A sudden clap of thunder and water poured like a pipe in the sky had just burst. I ran back home, soaked through to my skin. A few weeks later I left for college and I never saw Tack again.

Until, of course, today.

Chapter Eight

"Are you telling me there isn't a qualified chef within 20 miles of New Hope?" I ask Anita as she peers over her laptop at me.

"I'm telling you there isn't a qualified chef within 100 miles. Not with what you're paying."

I've been surveying my investment over the past few days and all of the capital I have left is going to have to go into renovating the eight rooms at the inn. They look like they haven't seen a guest since the inn was built in 1886. It's not a job I want or can do so I found a contractor who came in with a solid budget and a guarantee that he can have the rooms in decent shape by Labor Day. The rooms are far enough away from the dining room that any construction won't make a huge disturbance and this guy has enough experience with historic buildings that he won't need me to hold his hand. Although, if there weren't a wedding ring on his finger and he didn't have a vibe straighter than my bangs during a teenage flat iron phase, I would definitely hold more than his hand. In any event, there isn't a lot of cash to hire an experienced chef.

"Maybe I should get creative here and think about profit sharing as a way to entice a chef," I say, thinking out loud.

"Oh, sure," Anita says. For a split second I think I have won her approval. "Let's see, you are currently making a profit of zero so half of that would be... I don't have my calculator so let's just say approximately...zero!"

I'm getting used to Anita's barbs. No one talks to me like that but she's smart and has exceptional business skills. I need her so I have to put up with it. She's also got a sharp wit that impresses me, so that helps.

"There must be something else we could offer a chef..." I say, trying to come up with a solution.

Anita wheels away from her laptop to be right in front of me. "There is one thing," she says in an uncharacteristically sweet voice.

"What's that?" I ask, taking a swig of my still warm black coffee.

"Room and board," she says.

"The contractor is starting tomorrow. They'll be offline until the end of August."

"That's true," she says. She wheels to the other side of the kitchen and grabs the coffeepot then wheels closer to me and refills my cup. I'm immediately suspicious. "But the owner's suite is pretty big—two bedrooms, as I recall."

"It is," I say, putting my coffee down, "But I'm not sharing my apartment with a stranger." I'm desperate but the thought of having to wear a towel every time I take a hot shower after a workout is a bridge too far.

"No," Anita says, her voice still soft and singsong. "Not a stranger. Someone you know. Someone you used to know quite well."

"No way," I say firmly. "I thought we were figuring out options so I *don't* have to hire Tack."

"If you have a better way let me know, because the way I see it Tack is your only option." All of the sugar has completely evaporated from her voice. Welcome back, Anita.

I turn away from her and stare through the thick hand-blown crown window that looks out over Main Street. The lilac bush blurs through the glass and the lavender petals swirl in a way that makes them one with the leaves, street and sky.

When I bought this place I knew it would mean stirring up some old memories. I was prepared for that. But Tack? I'll never be prepared for that. After he broke my heart I took every feeling I had about him and shoved it so far down I was sure I would never have to see it again. But here those feelings are again, staring back at me in the wavy nineteenth century glass and it makes me nervous. No, I cannot have Tack working with me let alone living with me. It's impossible.

"Tack wants to start cooking at a real restaurant. He certainly has the talent and he's getting the training. I know the commute from the farm to culinary school is tough for him, so lodging here, with you, would be a big bonus. Big enough to make him take the job even."

Big bonus? I doubt that. When he left the kitchen yesterday that was the last I planned to see of him ever again and I'm pretty sure my performance made him feel the exact same way.

"Anita," I say, turning away from the window and leaning against the wall. "You don't understand. Tack and I...."

Anita lets out a laugh that makes her whole chair shake.

"What's so funny?" I ask.

"Obviously there is something going on between the two of you. But that's the past. It's time to start thinking about your present and future. Without Tack, I'm not sure this place has one. I've been doing this a long time. I know what chefs earn and I know what you can pay. I also know Tack is looking for a new place to stay."

"He is?"

"Yeah, he's living with his dad now."

That alone explains why he wants to move. But still, I don't want him to move in with me.

"Tack wants to be closer to town also. Vince, I'd tell you to consider all the options but there are no other options. It's Tack or nothing."

"But, Anita..." I start to whine and immediately catch myself. That is not who I am now. I can make hard decisions. I'm able to push my feelings aside in order to reach my goals and that is what I intend to do. Anita is right. Tack is part of my past and whatever happened back then is over. It doesn't have any impact on the current situation because I say it doesn't. That's what a man does. He takes control of his present and his future.

"Fine," I say firmly and flatly. Asking Tack to live and work here is the best decision for all involved. This will help me turn a profit so I can flip this place and get back to New York. I head upstairs to do some more unpacking. "Let me know what he says when you ask him," I say and hop onto the first step.

"Oh, hell no," Anita says and I freeze.

"I thought you wanted to hire Tack?" I say, continuing up the steps.

"I do. But I'm not going to make the offer. You are."

Boom. I lose my footing and trip over the next step, hitting the wall with the side of my body.

This is gonna hurt.

Chapter Nine

The view from the deck overlooking the river is magnificent. Manhattan is an island but even after living there for years I never really thought about the water surrounding it. The Delaware River, however, runs alongside New Hope, an always-present, loyal companion. It's the same river from before I left but it's also a completely different one. Water from the mountains miles away slowly descends to the headwaters and eventually rushes past me in this moment. It's never the same river twice.

I take one last swig of coffee and one last view of the muddy rushing water. The trees on the riverbank bend against the flow. They are just beginning to make good on their promise of a summer bloom.

My best chance to talk to Tack is after he is done at the

market and before he heads back to the farm, according to Anita. I'm about to ask Tack to work at my inn and move in with me. I might as well strip down to my underwear and attend the monthly board meeting of the firm I was let go from since that is also a recurring nightmare of mine.

Before I meet Tack I walk down Main to see if his favorite pretzel place is still there. I remember he had a thing for Mr. Pretzel's cinnamon and sugar twists. I'd buy one to split when he took a break from working on the fence that summer. At first, I would pretend that I just happened to be walking the property line of the farm and I just happened to be carrying his favorite treat with me. Then as the summer developed and we began to connect I brought them without any pretense whatsoever.

I cringe thinking about what a lovesick puppy I must have seemed to him. For a second, I change my mind about using the pretzels as a lure but once I'm close enough to smell the butter and sugar I can't change course. Making myself vulnerable to Tack is the last thing I want to do and if I have to do it, I'm going to need carbs.

As I approach the farmers market, pretzel twists in tow, I see that Tack is loading up his truck getting ready to leave. It's warmer than it was the other day so he's just wearing a loose T-shirt and his well-worn jeans that are so tight it makes it almost impossible not to stare at his groin and imagine what each bulge is hiding. His biceps pulse each time he lifts a crate onto his pickup. Mindlessly I grab a pretzel twist out of the bag as I stare at Tack's ass. I have no idea how long I'm staring when I'm suddenly forced back to earth.

"Did you move back here just for the pretzels?" Tack asks from across the sidewalk. Caught, I walk closer to him and pretend he didn't see what he just saw.

"These pretzels are your favorite. Not mine," I remind him.

He grabs the last crate from the table, puts it on the truck and then sits on the tailgate. I walk over to stand directly in front of him. He looks closely at what I've been munching.

"No, mine are the ones with the cheese filling. You have the sweet tooth. I'm salty."

Is he right? I thought we both liked them. "In any case," I say, regathering my thoughts so as not to appear weak. "This is an official peace offering." I hand him the uneaten one.

Tack doesn't say anything. He just looks at me. Silence can make me uncomfortable and I sometimes need to grip down to make it through but this silence with Tack is different. It's comfortable. We aren't saying anything in the moment but it feels like we are communicating.

"Vince," he says and I immediately feel appreciation that he is using the name I prefer. "You were stressed. You don't need to apologize for anything."

"I know I was kind of a dick."

"No, you weren't," he says. "You were a complete dick."

"Hey..." I say, about to stop him.

"But," he interrupts me. "I accept this pretzel, that you happen to be devouring, as a yeasty olive branch. But, Vince, I want to..." he starts but I stop him.

"Listen, Tack. I didn't come here to talk about the past. I'm here to talk about the present and the future."

He moves the last crate of radishes deeper into the bed of his truck and then closes the tailgate and leans against it. "Okay, I'm listening." He's calm but there is a small smile on his lips that makes me think he is eager to hear what I have to say.

"I have a business proposition for you."

"What? I didn't hear you. Did you say you want to proposition me? Vincent Amato, right here on Main Street?"

Tack has always been a smart-ass but he's never been a flirt. At least not with me and definitely not out in the open. We're at the farmers market where he knows every turnip that fell off the truck.

"A business proposition," I say. "*Business*. If you can't be serious then just forget it."

"I'm sorry. No jokes. I'm listening." His entire body changes and I can tell he is focused on what I'm saying like when I would tell him about the books I was reading.

"As you are well aware, The Hideaway Inn needs a chef for the dinner service. We are reframing much of the P&L statement for the enterprise."

"English, please."

He wears me down.

"I need a chef. I can't pay much but I can provide room and board." I don't want to reveal that I know he's split from Evie. Not yet, at least.

Tack suddenly looks very interested. "One of the rooms? At the inn. Here in New Hope?"

"Yes," I say. I should tell him that it means actually sharing the upstairs apartment with me but I leave out that detail since I'm dreading the awkwardness.

He looks at me with very wide eyes. "Vince, before we discuss that, there are a few things I need to tell you. First, you brought up Evie the other day and the truth is we're divorced. Also I think you should know..."

"Stop," I say. The only way I can manage this untenable situation is if I draw a firm line here.

"But Vince..."

"Your personal life is your personal life. This is not about that at all. This is about the inn." Once I have made myself clear I continue. "We would have much of the same staff in terms of service and food prep. Anita has managed to keep the line cooks and bus boys, et cetera, but we need someone to chef. Anita thinks you can do it."

"And what about you?"

"I can't cook. It would be like a Charlie Brown Thanksgiving with toast and jelly beans."

"No, I mean, do *you* think I can do it?" He looks at me squarely. All his charm and charisma stands to the side as he bites his lower lip, waiting for an answer. I assume he's asking me in a professional context. Could my personal opinion be that important to him?

I've been going on Anita's word and the fact that there doesn't seem to be any other option. I haven't really thought about whether he has the talent or not. I wish I could say that I haven't thought about him since I left over a decade ago but that isn't true. I thought about him a lot and not just when I had my dick in my hand. But the Tack I thought about is not the one standing before me waiting for approval. Tack used to seem impenetrable to me—a compelling mystery I enthusiastically tried to unravel without success. After I left I assumed Tack's life would progress in entirely the way it had been planned for him. Culinary school is the last place I expected him to be but I guess "Most Popular" isn't a skill set on LinkedIn.

"I thought your plan was to work your dad's farm. I had no idea you changed course," I say.

"It was, but my dad is getting on in age. He's never been exactly a live and let live kind of guy."

"I remember." Mr. O'Leary was a deacon or something at the church they went to. Their church preached a form of Christianity that considered anything beyond reading the Bible and breathing to be a sin, and I'm not sure breathing wasn't on the list. I kept my distance from his dad but Tack told me plenty of stories about strict punishments and unreasonable expectations.

"My brothers moved away and my dad has a few farmhands that keep the animals going and produce a few crops that we sell here. He's sold off some of the land and rented some to farmers. He has nurses around the clock or members of the congregation see to him. He doesn't need me. I've made some adjustment in my plans. You're not the only one that can change," he says. It's not a challenge; it's more of an invitation—like he wants me to find out more.

He grabs a small bucket that looks like it has leftover vegetable parts in it. I see browned radish greens and an oddly shaped carrot. "Come help me feed the ducks," he says and starts walking toward the shoreline of the river.

I panic. I look over at the small hut with a freehand painting of Donald Duck and the words "Quack Shack." Tourists buy bags of food for whatever web-footed scaven-

gers are in the area. "It's sold out," I say. "No more bags."
It doesn't say that at all but I'm hoping he believes me.

"What are you talking about? Anyway, I've got scraps
right here. Let's go."

He starts walking and I freeze. He looks at me and then
realizes why I'm so terrified.

"Don't worry. Mrs. Waddles isn't there. Old girl has
been gone a while."

My body relaxes and I follow him toward the sound of
gently lapping water. The ducks are waiting for Tack and
as soon as they see him they gather around and wait for
his scraps. It's the high school lunch room all over again.

Even though I believe Tack, I look closely for Mrs. Waddles. I hated that feathered spawn of Satan and she hated
me. We had a whole thing going on for years. She once
bit my finger so hard it bled. The very memory of Mrs.
Waddles is enough to make me never want to return here.
That duck was a complete shithead.

Tack offers me the bucket and a few ducks that don't
seem to know about my long-standing feud with their
cousin approach me. I feed them fearfully but without in-
cident and hope Tack doesn't see my trepidation. From
the riverbank, the trellis bridge that connects New Hope
to Lambertville rumbles calmly as cars transfer from one
state to the other. The aqua-green patina glows against the
dirty brown river in the afternoon sun.

I take a limp piece of celery out of the bucket, stare at
the duck to avoid eye contact with Tack and ask, "So what
made you get interested in cooking?" I should just ask him
directly—look him in the eye like a man. I'm offering him

a job and this is a question any employer would ask. But I'm not asking as a business owner. As much as I hate myself for it, I'm asking for me. I want to know.

Tack walks over to a bench on the river walk and sits down. I sit next to him but make sure we don't touch. I don't trust what that physical connection would do to me. I'm also careful to keep an eye on these ducks.

"I love the farm. I still do. It's just that being on the farm is isolating." Tack stares out at the water. "We work the fields, tend to the animals and it's all connected to the land and that felt great. In fact, for most of my life it did more than that."

He stops, picks a stone from under his foot and throws it so it skips across the water.

"More than what?" I ask.

"It made me feel protected from the world. Of course, my dad always made it seem like the world was out to destroy itself and everyone who didn't follow his rules."

"I never thought you needed protection from anything." The world always seemed to be made for Tack. Whatever he wanted seemed to appear magically in front of him— popularity, good looks, athleticism.

"I mean, I did. Well, I do. Doesn't everybody need that?"

"No, I don't. Not anymore," I say with conviction. I want him to know I don't need anyone to protect me anymore. I protect myself and I do it more fiercely than anyone else ever could.

"I can see that," Tack says and he looks at me but the glance is too quick to know if it is filled with admiration, respect or something else altogether. "But then things changed. I changed. I wanted to be out in the world."

I want to ask him *how* he'd changed but it's too cloying a question. I just told him how I no longer need protection. I can't retreat on that by demonstrating neediness.

"I started doing less at the farm and more at the market. I would talk to people buying our produce. They'd tell me what they were planning to cook. I listened and started trying things at home. I got pretty good at it and then I wanted to share my food with other people. If I used ingredients from my farm or the farms I knew, it would be like bringing that private part out and making it public."

He picks up another rock and throws it toward the water but this one doesn't skip at all, it just sinks to the bottom of the river.

The sky turns cloudy and a wind rolls off that river that brings a chill to the air. The river walk is empty and we just sit on the bench staring straight ahead, not saying anything. I want to turn and look at him so I can see into his eyes and feel even more of his story or touch his arm or move his blond bangs off his face but I fight every urge I have and stare straight ahead. I watch the sun's rays refract on the water like a river disco ball until a cloud moves across the sky and flattens the sharpness of the light.

"Yes," I say quietly.

"What?"

"Yes. I believe you can do it."

The clouds shift again and the sun reappears, dancing on the water. I feel Tack turn his head toward me and, without thinking, I turn my head to meet his and our eyes connect.

"Thank you," he says. "I won't let you down." He grabs the now empty bucket and walks back to the market. I stay and stare at the water rushing under the bridge as it splits around the pylons holding up the bridge and then comes back together on the other side.

It's never the same river twice.

Chapter Ten

Tack

Pesto with the basil from the sunny herb garden across from the bend in the river. Mushrooms from the guy across from me at the farmers market. Cheese from the goat farm just outside of town. A list of ingredients starts entering my mind from every direction.

I can't wait to start designing menus, surveying the local food chain for the best ingredients and thinking about how to blend different seasonal flavors. I'm not going to disappoint Vinny—I mean Vince. I'm not going to disappoint Vince. The commute has been rough but it's been the only way to pursue my passion and still be a part of the life of the most important person in the world to me: my kid.

I drive down Main Street toward the more residential part of town where Evie lives in an apartment in one of the massive Victorians that jewel the tree-lined streets. After the divorce she got a job at a clothing store in town and a girlfriend named Ines who teaches Portuguese at the local university. It made sense for her to be in town and we save money with me staying at the farm even though I'd rather be closer.

Evie and I were clinging to each other for a lot of the same reasons. She was terrified by her attraction to women and I didn't want to deal with my same-sex feelings, but once we had a kid we both realized we needed to be better role models and found a way to be honest with each other. Even though we've been divorced a few years we're closer now than we ever were. Partly because we've finally been honest with each other and partly because we happen to co-parent the best kid in the world.

I turn up Old Mill Road and find a spot right in front of the blue and yellow meticulously maintained gingerbread where Evie rents the back apartment. Ines hasn't moved in yet but it's only a matter of time.

I hear arguing in the backyard and immediately open the picket fence to go behind the house and see what's going on.

"Jules, I told you. You can wear the purple T-shirt with the dinosaur or the red one with the truck but you have to wear your pants." Evie sounds like she is on her last nerve.

"What's going on?" I make sure my tone is not elevated or agitated in any way. I hate hearing them argue. I don't like confrontation.

Jules has their back toward me and is holding one of their favorite dresses. "But, please, Mom. I don't want to wear that. I want to wear this," they say and hold up the dress.

"Great," Evie sighs. "Reinforcements."

"What's going on?" I repeat as calmly as possible.

Before she can answer my kid sees me and runs over and hugs my legs. "Dad!" It's like a magic word that makes my heart overflow with love and pride. "Can I wear this today? Please. I was thinking about it all last night and it's really the perfect day to wear it."

They hold up an orange dress with purple glittery tulle for a skirt. It's something a ballerina in a circus in outer space might wear. It's silly, and flamboyant and wonderful—just like Jules.

"Wow!" I say. "That's amazing. Are you going tightrope walking on Mars?"

Jules looks at me like I have come up with the most fantastic idea in the world.

"Yes," they say and go back to running around the backyard, playing without a care in the world.

Once Jules is out of earshot Evie explains. "It's this screwed up camp. I know we interviewed them and thought everything would be okay but the director called and they said he has to wear pants every day. He's been wearing overalls and some pants but today he has his heart set on that dress. I have no idea why." I put my arm around Evie. It's clear she has been through it and her eyes look red from tears.

"They. They have their heart set on that dress," I say as softly as possible.

Evie sits down and puts her head in her hand. She looks like she might start crying again. "You're right," she says. "They." We started trying to use a more neutral pronoun with Jules a few months ago when they requested it. All of the books and articles we read said allowing them to choose was the right thing to do. I don't want to force them into a gender choice and I also want them to be whoever they need to be. I was never allowed any choices growing up. I don't want my kid to feel limited by the life they were born into the way I did. Maybe Jules will be a fashion designer or a coal miner or pickle briner. I don't care. I want Jules to be happy.

Maybe letting Jules choose what they are called is the right thing to do, maybe it's messing them up. Maybe other parents would do it differently, I have no idea, but being a parent involves a lot of not knowing.

"This ignorant director. Why can't Jules express themselves as they want? What does it matter what they wear?"

"Um, because the director is an ignorant ass." I walk over to the empty chair next to her and sit down. "Let's just pull them out."

"Who's going to watch them? It's not like we can leave them with your dad."

Evie almost never mentions my dad since she tries to keep her distance from him as much as possible. Jules is almost a stranger to him and, in most ways, even though I've been living in the room next to his for a couple years, so am I.

"What about that other camp closer to Doylestown? Chapman Creek Day."

"Tack, you know we can't afford that. It's much more progressive and much more expensive. Inclusive philosophy, exclusive price tag."

Jules is dancing on the other side of the yard. They spin, jump up in the air and then land on the ground. We both have our eyes on them as we talk.

"Who knew not being an asshole would cost more money," I say and it lightens the mood enough to make her laugh. "I can watch him later this afternoon after I get back from the farm."

"And I can get Patricia to switch some shifts for me this week until we figure it out." Jules moves to the sandbox and starts playing with their favorite dump truck, filling it with sand and letting it cascade out. Jules has no idea that they are "supposed" to like one thing or the other. They love dump trucks and tutus with equal enthusiasm. "Wait, what are you doing here? Shouldn't you be at the farm?"

"On my way but I wanted to stop here first to let you both know that I got a job in town. Cooking, actually, and it comes with room and board so I'll just be a short ride instead of down at the farm across the river."

"Jules will love that," she says enthusiastically. She is genuinely happy for me and it feels good to be able to do something that will benefit all of us.

"Wait," she says, moving forward in her chair. "Is this with Vinny? At Vinny's place?" I told her about his return the other day and I could tell it made her radar go up. When I came out to her as bi I confessed that I first realized I had these feelings that summer with Vince. Of course, this came as no surprise to her but it was the first time I'd said it out loud to anyone. Even though I was with Evie in high school it was Vince who captured my heart. It was always Vince and I always had a hunch she knew it.

"Do not call him Vinny. He goes by Vince now." Driving with him in my truck last week is an image I can't seem to shake and it makes a smile move across my lips with a gentle but unstoppable force. This does not go unnoticed by Evie.

"Maybe the two of you..."

"Evie, don't go there," I say firmly even though that and designing a menu are almost the only things I've been thinking about. "Things are different now. He's different," I say, hoping to throw her off the scent for a bit.

"You're different too," she says, taking my hand. "He wanted you to accept who you are and you've done that. You're out. You're even out to your dad and I know that wasn't easy."

"No, it wasn't." My dad knows but we've never actually spoken about it and I don't suspect we ever will. But at least he knows.

Jules comes over to us and says, "Can I go inside? I have an idea for a story and I want to write it down with my glitter crayons before I forget. It's about a dump truck that fights fires but gets into a fight with an electric toothbrush and a tablecloth."

"Sure," Evie says and gives them a kiss on the cheek.

As soon as they are gone we both let out a laugh. This kid's imagination will solve world hunger or create a binge-worthy reality show one day. It's hard to know. One thing

I do know is that I'm not going to let anybody punish their creativity.

"We have to get them into Chapman Creek," I say.

"This job is great but doesn't sound like it will bring in enough money." She's right. I think for a second. We pull in just enough to cover our expenses and anything outside the budget means carefully saving. When I needed a set of professional knives for school I had to save for months until I was able to make the purchase.

And then I realize: "My knives," I say.

She shakes her head. "The Wusthof? No, no way. You saved for months and months and you need them. You said they make you feel like a real chef. No way." They do. A good knife can be like an extension of a chef's hand. Not only did I save for months, I also painstakingly researched each blade so I was sure I was getting the very best I could find.

But in the end they're just knives and Jules comes first.

"I'm sure there are knives at The Hideaway."

"But you need them for class," she insists.

"I'm just taking Restaurant Operations this summer. It's all spreadsheets and numbers." I should say I'm *retaking* it since I failed it this spring. I can't seem to make those columns on the spreadsheet do what I want. "I'll figure out the fall classes later," I say.

"But..." She goes to make another argument but I don't let her. I hold up my hand to signal I've made my decision.

"It's settled. I'll call the Chapman camp and tell them we will have the deposit tomorrow and you call the assholes camp and tell them they're assholes."

A wicked smile forms across Evie's mouth. "With pleasure." Evie used to be a total bitch to anyone who threatened the tight circle she built around herself in high school and, while she is totally reformed, I do rely on her bringing back that part every now and then.

"Hey, Jules," I yell back into the apartment. "Come on out here and show me and your mom how the skirt on that dress twirls when you spin."

Chapter Eleven

I see Tack's truck pull into the small parking lot. For a
second I return to the idea of me taking on the chef's role
then I remember I had a protein shake and string cheese for
lunch. This is a business arrangement. He is simply someone I have hired to do a job. He's no different than Steve,
the contractor I hired to renovate the rooms. Still, when
I met with Steve last week I didn't make sure to exfoliate,
trim my facial hair and wear a shirt that showed off all the
best parts of my upper body. I remind myself that I'm here
to turn a profit and get out of this town and back to the
city where there are no memories of being Skinny Vinny.
I squeeze my hands into fists and feel my muscles tighten.
I'm not going to let Tack get me off track.

From the window, I watch him unload a few crates of

produce and a large duffel from his truck. He's wearing a tight, crisp white T-shirt and a pair of sharp khakis. I've seen a lot of handsome men in my life but there is something about Tack that is beyond anything else. He has this charismatic inner life that makes everyone around him want to be with him. At least that's how it makes me feel. Made me feel. *Made*, I repeat to myself and hit my forehead.

What have I done? Inviting Tack to work and live with me under the same roof is insane. After arranging all the details we decided he would cook a dinner for me to test a few menu items and then he could settle into the suite. I still haven't been completely up front about the living arrangement but I'm hoping after dinner a meteor will hit town and solve most of my problems.

Tack opens the back door, walks in and puts down his stuff. He grabs an apron from a crate and pulls it over his head, tying the strings in the back. I'm not really into bondage but something about seeing him struggle to tie the knot with his hands behind his back makes me reconsider the fetish. "I hope you're ready for the best dinner of your entire life, Vinny," he says with a big smile.

"It's Vince," I say firmly. "How many times do I have to tell you? I have zero confidence you can remember the orders if you can't remember my name."

"Okaaaay," Tack says slowly, not reacting to my childish outburst. "Maybe someone is hangrier than I thought. I'm glad I brought a few extra servings, Vince. Or do you prefer Mr. Amato?"

"Vince is fine. Look, it just took me a long time to…" I

stop myself before pouring out all of my feelings the way Vinny would.

"I understand," Tack says. "People have the right to be called whatever they want to be called. Let me tell you about the menu for our test run tonight. We start with a salad of local watercress and baby kale. I make this very simple vinaigrette with a hint of maple syrup from a place in the Poconos. The main course is a fettuccini Alfredo with mushrooms from my family's farm. For dessert I have a lemon and lavender sorbet with lavender from Langford Lavender Farm near Washington's Crossing."

"Are we eating or going on a field trip of Eastern Pennsylvania?" I ask, the sarcasm dripping like the maple syrup from the trees in the Poconos.

"Local cuisine and simple preparation is very popular right now," he says and hands me a copy of the menu that he wrote out by hand.

I look it over quickly. "Haven't you forgotten something?"

"I thought about adding some balsamic vinegar to the salad but I think the greens have so much flavor right now. I don't think they need anything." His voice cracks a bit and reveals his vulnerability. "What's missing?"

"I'm not talking about the salad. I'm talking about meat. Protein. Where's the food?"

"This is food. There is plenty of protein in this menu to satisfy anyone. Anyway, aren't you still a vegan?"

"I was never a vegan," I say, looking at him defiantly. Our eyes connect for a second longer than I would like and I shift my focus.

"Of course you were. Senior year of high school you survived on sunflower seeds that you kept in the pocket of that black hoodie with the Dead Kennedys patches on it."

"Oh yeah," I say, remembering that hoodie. I found it in a thrift store and wore it every day of school whether it was below freezing or sweltering. It was about three sizes too big for my rail-thin frame and when I put the hood up, it hid me from the world. And I do remember sunflower seeds being a permanent fixture of those pockets and vowing never to eat meat. But how does he remember what I wore and what I ate? It's not like he ever hung out with me at school after that summer he built the fence. I became invisible to him. "I remember the hoodie but I was never a vegan," I say just to challenge him and stay on my guard. "And it doesn't matter because I certainly eat meat now. My trainer would lose it if I told him I was vegan. All our work to build muscle relies on a high protein diet."

Tack starts pulling vegetables out of the crate, including a bright red basket of fresh strawberries that's so fragrant the scent should be bottled. "Yeah," he says, taking a second to look at me, "I can tell you've put on a few pounds of muscle."

His tone is polished nonchalance but I can tell he sees my gains. Let him look and see what he missed a chance on. He continues unpacking the groceries and doesn't look up at me. "Very impressive," he says, rolling his eyes.

Now I'm getting pissed. I've worked hard for this body and it usually makes guys roll over and present their asses to me without hesitation. In fact, some rip my clothes off and beg. How dare he brush off my hard work? "Well, excuse me if I don't have the perfectly toned physique that comes from hard farm labor."

Tack puts down the pan he just took out from the cabinet. "Perfectly toned? So you think my body is perfectly toned?" Tack smiles at me, knowing his teasing is getting to me.

Crap. Why did I have to say that? It just came out of me. It's accurate but I would rather have used a more neutral, less sexually charged phrase. "I didn't say that your body is perfectly toned," I snap at him. Of course I did but I'm using denial as a strategy for dealing with the slip.

"Yes, you did! You said my body is perfectly toned. That's what you said. Admit it," he says, his grin showing total playfulness. This is not a challenge to a duel; it's an invitation to play. But I don't accept. We aren't kids. I'm not going to arm wrestle him for winner. Although I would absolutely win and the things I would do to him would destroy him with pleasure. I'd slam his arm to the table and declare my victory by pulling off that apron and making sure those khakis are balled up on the floor in a few seconds. But I catch myself and respond with force.

"Grow up, Tack," I say calmly without too much bite. My tone is serious and professional. I need to make sure I keep up my walls or else this entire situation will explode. "You aren't a child and neither am I. I hired you to do a job and I expect it to be done. It's been a long day and I'm hungry so you had better find a way to turn this leftover rabbit chow into something edible. I'll be in the dining room."

I walk out of the kitchen and as soon as the door swings closed behind me I sit down to stop myself from vibrating with anger and lust.

Chapter Twelve

That night I suffer through the most torturous meal of my entire life. Each bite, each morsel is exquisite. The salad is a completely unexpected combination of sweet and tangy flavors that are so delicious that I only want to eat three courses of the salad until the fettuccini comes out. Then I want nothing but the creamy, luxurious noodles and the sharp, tender mushroom in my mouth. My stomach is smiling but my exterior is ice. It's been a very unexpected sensual experience. Tack's preparation of the delectable food that has passed through my lips would be considered foreplay in most situations but I won't slip and allow him to see that it generates pleasure throughout my whole body.

I remain silent during the meal but I catch Tack looking up from his plate to see if I'm having any reaction to his cooking. I'm like a robot eating his food and I can tell it's killing him. Ha. I'll never let him see me at his mercy again. A bell goes off in the kitchen. Tack gets up and says, "I have to check on dessert." I shrug my shoulders and I can tell he is chagrinned by my response.

I wait for the kitchen door to swing shut and then I pick up my plate and lick up every drop of the remaining sauce.

He returns with the prettiest dessert I have ever seen. A delicate saucer with a rose pattern holds a perfect yellow ball of sorbet that has tiny pieces of rind dotting the surface. A smatter of sugared purple blossoms cling to a drizzle of honey that oozes over the frozen globe. It's springtime on a dish.

My eyes widen as he puts the dessert down in front of me. Damn. I blew my cover. "You like?" he asks earnestly. "The sorbet needs to be served at the exact right melting point. Isn't the honey amazing? I got it from a woman in Pipersville."

"It's adequate," I say, swallowing a delicious mouthful and wondering if I can sneak back into the kitchen in the middle of the night to steal another taste of any leftovers. "The whole meal was adequate," I say, my voice unwavering. I can't help toying with his insecurity.

"Just adequate?" he asks. His eyes are in full puppy dog mode.

"No, not just adequate. More than adequate…" I watch his eyes open in anticipation. "The food was…what's the right word…*fine*. Yes," I say. "The food was fine." He is crestfallen. "But a restaurant isn't just about food. It's a business."

I push my dish away from me like I don't want any more and I see his eyes study the puddle of sunshine I've very reluctantly left behind.

"A restaurant has to make deals with vendors and suppliers and form business to business relationships. Wholesale operations work because you buy most of your goods from one place and that bulk order earns you a discount and that increases profitability. I'm not sure some lady in Pipersville is able to compete like that."

"A restaurant isn't like other businesses. It's not a competition. At least not the way I see it. People come to a place like this to eat great food but also to be part of the community. To eat the food that is grown in the area and cooked by people from the community. Isn't that what you want to do? That takes time to build."

I don't tell him that I plan to flip this place to FunTyme Inc. as soon as possible and use the money to get back to New York so I can start making some real investments. I have no intention of being here a second longer than I need to. But I need to get this place open and start showing some money in the cash flow statement so I let him think I'm here for the long haul.

"It's getting late and we have a lot to do tomorrow. Let's get some sleep," I say, cutting off the discussion.

"I can finish cleaning up in the morning. Just show me which guest room is mine." Tack gets up and goes back through to the kitchen. I follow him and he grabs his duffel and stands at the foot of the stairs.

"I didn't really get a chance to explain the arrangement the other day."

"Explain what?" he asks.

I breathe in and out quickly through my nostrils. I don't know why I'm getting so nervous about telling Tack that we're sharing the owner's suite. This is a business decision that benefits us both. Nothing more, nothing less.

"The last owner let the guest rooms deteriorate. I've hired a contractor to renovate all of them. The restaurant is the money maker. The rooms can happen later."

Tack looks puzzled but not angry. "So where do I bunk?"

I point straight up and we take the back stairs from the kitchen.

"I didn't know there were guest rooms up here."

"There aren't," I say.

"So I'm sleeping in the attic?"

"No, it's a fully furnished space. It's actually in very good condition. Gorgeous views of the river on one side and town on the other."

"So what's the problem? As long as it has a working bathroom I'm in. I just want to shower off the day and hit the hay."

"There's only one space up here. We'll be sharing the owner's suite," I say as if it's the most natural thing in the world. I open the door to the apartment and dart through the small living room to open his door. I want to make it clear he will have his own bedroom. "This room is yours. The kitchen is small but in good condition. A few things need repairs. Some of the windows won't open and the bathroom door won't close all the way but they're on Steve's list."

Tack drops his duffel on the floor just beyond the door.

"So…we're roommates," he says, placing his hand on my shoulder. The feel of his body touching mine makes me lose composure. It was hard enough staying calm when he was filling my mouth with such incredible food but this pushes me over the edge.

"No, no, no, no," I babble. "You have your own room over there and mine is way, way over here." I take about three steps from one side of the small space to the other.

I feel a drip rolling down my forehead and I can see that Tack's shirt is damp from perspiration. His sweat is the result of hard work. Mine is another situation entirely. "As long as I can take a shower, I don't care," he says and moves his duffel to the bedroom. "Do you want to take a shower first?" he asks.

"No, I will in the morning."

"Good, because I need to get in there," he says and peels off his damp T-shirt to reveal his smooth perfectly toned chest. There isn't as much of a valley between his pecs as mine but he is definitely muscular from years of hard work on the farm. A thin layer of perspiration across his chest makes his whole upper body glisten. I'm having difficulty releasing myself from the state of suspended animation his half-naked body has created. "Is there something wrong with the bathroom?" he asks.

"I mean, the door needs to be fixed but it all works. Why?"

"You're blocking the entrance like there's something in there I shouldn't see."

The only thing that shouldn't be seen is his half-naked body. I forgot that Tack was never the kind of guy to be self-conscious about showing some skin. He was always the first to strip off his shirt or get down to his underwear to take a swim in the river. I wore T-shirts three sizes too big for my stick-thin body, covered in a sweatshirt that could have doubled as a parachute. I break out of my stupor and step aside to let him pass.

"All yours." I walk to my bedroom door, which is directly across the living space from the bathroom. "Good night," I say as I almost close my bedroom door behind me. Once I'm in my room I keep the lights off.

What is it about being around Tack that makes me act like a teenager? I am a grown man. I should collapse on the bed and go to sleep. Instead I quietly look through the door I left cracked open just enough.

Tack turns on the water and then the show begins. He unbuckles his pants but catches a glimpse of his face in the mirror and runs one of his hands over his face and then past his forehead to brush his bangs back. He's not preening. He never did that. Tack has always been comfortable in his skin. Now even with all this muscle and minimal body fat I still feel like a twerp in a locker room. Sure, I strut around like I own the place but it's all bravado, not like Tack who is naturally easy in his body.

The hot water mixes with the cool night air and steam forms around the shower. Tack takes another sample of the temperature with his hand and then uses both hands to unbutton his khakis. In a single swift motion, his pants drop to the floor and his dick swings freely.

I like looking at dicks as much as any gay man but let's face it, most of them look about the same, some longer, some thicker, but only occasionally do you come across one that is worth writing home about. Tack's dick deserves a ticker tape parade made out of all the letters that should be written about his cock. It's not just that it's long, it's actually pretty. It's weird to describe a dick as pretty since an objective opinion would point out they actually look like sea creatures but Tack's dick is actually pretty. No, not pretty—it's handsome.

Now that he is naked he grabs some soap from the shelf next to the sink and gives his dick one good fluff before turning around and giving me a perfect view of his sculpted ass. I'm intently focused on his backside until my eyes travel up his body and notice him looking right through the open door toward my bedroom.

Damn. He knows I'm watching. I immediately cover my eyes and jump away from the door. Of course, he didn't seem to be in any hurry to pull the shower curtain closed. I hear him turn off the water. He walks out of the bathroom with a towel wrapped around his tight body and comes right over to my bedroom door before I am able to close it.

"Good night, Vince," he says with a cocky grin and waves his fingers at me through the crack. He knew I was watching the whole time. The towel struggles to stay in place as his convex ass cheeks flex with each step back to his room. I'm distracted by it just long enough to delay the feeling of humiliation by a few seconds.

He shuts his door and I seal mine as tightly as I can. He may be a few yards away and behind two closed doors but I can still feel Tack's presence as deeply as if he were standing right in front of me.

Chapter Thirteen

Brightness penetrates my eyelids. I want to sleep more so I reach over to the nightstand to grab the remote for the blinds. One simple squeeze and the entire room will turn from being a few inches from the sun to the dark side of the moon. I reach out but there is no remote. My hands explore more and I realize there is no nightstand. It all suddenly comes down on me. I'm not in my sleek penthouse over Gramercy Park; I'm in a dilapidated inn in New Hope, Pennsylvania. Then the bigger reality hits me. I'm roommates with Tack O'Leary.

I open my bedroom door and tiptoe across the living room to look in Tack's room. He's gone. The tension that has gripped my upper body releases. He's left some coffee on the stove and I pour myself a cup and grab my phone to check for what I missed while I was sleeping. A few of the apps have messages from guys wanting to get banged but I ignore those and open the three text messages from Barry. The first says, "Call me." The second says, "CALL ME!" and the third says, "Call me asshole!"

I dial and hear a foreign ring which means Barry could be anywhere in the world.

"Do you have any idea what fucking time it is here?"

I forgot he's in Tokyo. FunTyme has been buying up mom and pop noodle shops and Barry is the numbers guy there. He's a loose cannon but a valuable asset. "Sorry, are you in bed?" I ask.

"Not yet but I've got a twenty-eight-year-old guy waiting in my room at the Park Hyatt so let's make this quick." Barry is in his late forties, married with two kids. He's from Staten Island and made a small fortune in private sanitation. His great head with numbers turned a small fortune into a huge fortune. He acts like a frat boy, still spends summers on the truck doing the sanitation rounds, and sounds like a rougher version of Andrew Dice Clay. After spending a few decades raising a family he's catching up for lost time making his search for dick a full-time job. The only catch is no one is supposed to know he's into guys on the side. It's the worst kept secret in real estate finance. "I had an opening so I pitched the Hide and Seek Inn before I left."

"The Hideaway," I correct him.

"Yeah, whatever. They love the location according to their demographics. It's definitely on their radar. But look, you gotta have that place showing some activity. They won't buy old dogs. And you got to do this by Labor Day.

They have a group of investors and delays make them nervous. Labor Day is the deadline. You got it?"

"Got it." It's only the beginning of June so that should be enough time if I'm focused. I wanted to be out of here by then anyway. "Not a problem. Now go have some fun. Just don't have another heart attack. I don't want to fly to Tokyo to get you to the ER. Again."

"Hey, that wasn't my fault. If you had seen that guy's dick you would have had a heart attack too. And you only had to travel like twenty blocks. Geez."

"Goodbye, Barry."

"Should have a good story for you very soon," he says and hangs up.

I wonder if I should make a reservation for Labor Day weekend on Fire Island. Looks like I'll have something to celebrate. I take a quick shower and head downstairs with more determination than ever to start making this place turn a profit. The sooner I'm in the black the sooner I'm back.

When I walk into the kitchen both Tack and Anita have their heads buried in their laptops. I walk over to the coffee and pour myself another cup. "I want us to open for dinner next week." After my call with Barry, I'm hot to get this moving.

"Anita and I are still figuring that out."

"This isn't your office on Wall Street. You can't just snap your fingers and the restaurant reopens for dinner," Anita scolds me. My first reaction is to say, "Of course I can," but instead I grab a chair from the table and sit down.

"I've got some ideas."

"You do, do you?" Anita sighs. "So you're a chef now? When was the last time you cooked a meal?" Anita asks, giving me a shrewd look.

"I've eaten in some of the best restaurants in the world. Cabaña las Lilas in Buenos Aires, The Savoy in London and they know me by name at Le Bernardin."

Anita points to her blank expression. "Do you see this? This is my unimpressed look."

"Hey, I've got an idea," Tack says. "Why don't you take a walk around town and Anita and I will keep doing what we're doing? This afternoon we'll meet up and you guys can go over the marketing and budget and you and I can review the menu together to see how soon we can open."

I have a sudden flash of his naked body entering the shower. In an attempt to tear the image from my mind I decide to let them do their jobs and head out of the inn. I do have a visit I should pay.

When I was a kid, New Hope was an open secret. A place to be hidden and seen all at the same time. Everyone knew that the town had a queer history but that history lived peacefully alongside the narrative that New Hope was also just another picturesque river town. I could visit without having to confront my sexuality in ways I wasn't ready for. It wasn't an inclusive paradise but it was better than any local alternative.

Radley's Bookstore is in the center of New Hope, next to the Bucks County Playhouse and across from an antique shop. Reading used to be an escape for me. I could tune out the world as long as I had a book with me. My mother used to say, "When you have a book with you, you're never bored and you're never lonely." But once college started I was reading for classes and by the time I finished my MBA and started working, it didn't seem like there was any time to read for pleasure.

I walk farther away from the inn and toward Radley's. Most of New Hope has remained the same but there are a few changes. Wax On which sold candles and incense is now Cupcake-a-rooni and what I think was a women's clothing store called Rebekah's Remarkables is now a pet shop called Paw Time. The front sidewalk of The Beautiful Things Shoppe is still crowded with rusted antiques that have been sitting out there since I was kid. I have no idea how that place stays in business.

Radley's looks exactly the same. A two-story stone and stucco building with bright fire engine red double doors flanked by two large square-paned bay windows. The one on the left has book displays and the one on the right has the register and two overstuffed wingback chairs covered in a floral print for customers who want to jump right into their purchase or have a leisurely preview of a first chapter. Two cherry trees guard the sidewalk, their blooms in full regalia.

I decide to take a risk. I cross the street quickly and open the door to the bookstore. The familiar bells alerting the entrance of a customer ring and I quickly move past the entrance into the stacks.

I'm safely in nonfiction when it hits me. The smell. Old paper mixed with sandalwood and jasmine. I take a deep breath and look around at the shelves of neatly arranged books.

I hear the clicking of heels and realize someone is coming toward me. The clicking heels get closer until she is right in front of me.

"Well, Vinny Amato. I was wondering when you would come over to see your old friend." She holds her arms opens wide. I immediately recognize her. I knew she could never sell the bookstore. I walk over to her open arms and accept the hug like it's something I've been waiting years for. As I hug her she whispers in my ear, "It's Toula now."

"You look fantastic," I say. I step back and survey the full bosom, flowing peasant skirt and bright auburn-plum hair with gray streaks that hangs to her shoulders. "By the way, it's Vince now. Not Vinny."

"I heard," she says with the same knowing smile she has always had. "Let me get you a cup of tea and I'll explain," she says. "Chamomile and mint still okay?"

I haven't had herbal tea for years. By this time of the late morning I've usually poured at least a few shots of fine espresso down my throat but right now her homemade blend of chamomile buds and mint from her patio garden sounds perfect.

"Sure," I say, smiling.

"There's a copy of a book of poetry by a new trans poet on the table next to your chair. The cover is dreadful but the poems are inspired. You dive in and I'll be over in a jiffy. I've been waiting for you to come in."

I do as I am told although I wonder how Toula knew I was back in town. I wind myself back through the shelves of books to the seating area by the north bay window. The same easy chair I sat in as a teen waits for me. Toula always preferred a wooden rocker for herself because she said it was easier to get in and out of in case a customer came in.

I sink into the cushions and they welcome me back like old friends. I see the book on the small side table next to the chair. White words announce *Disquisitive* on the front and the cover truly is horrible. I think about opening it up to read a few poems but poetry can take a lot of work and, for me, it was sometimes like a hallucinogenic drug. Just a few lines in and my mind would explode with thoughts or images. I don't need that right now. I need to stay in control.

I hear the rattling of cups and saucers as Toula approaches and hands me my teacup. "Here you are, dear," she says. I take a sip of the pale yellow liquid and for a second, I'm a teen again, but I push the present into place to stop any flood of memories.

Toula settles into her chair and then stares at me. "It sure took you long enough to stop by."

"How did you know?" I ask sheepishly.

"Well, two things really. First, I noticed that handsome Tack O'Leary coming in and out of The Hideaway."

I immediately look down. Toula knows exactly how I feel about him. Rather, how I felt about him. Past tense. "And the second?" I ask, trying to move the subject away from Tack as soon as possible.

"Full disclosure. That little firecracker, Anita, is not only your house manager. She's also my wife." If there was ever a time to do a spit take it would be now but instead I manage to choke down my tea. "Isn't she the most mar-

velous creature you have ever met?" She picks up the rose-
patterned teapot and pours more of the steaming golden
liquid into my chipped teacup painted with tiny violets.
The familiar smell of steeped chamomile blossoms is pun-
gent yet comforting.

"It's clear you think so," I say and this time my tea goes
down easily. Toula is happy. There is no mistaking it and
it only takes me a second to understand how she and Anita
could balance each other. Toula tells me about meeting
Anita and their honeymoon to Niagara Falls after what she
calls "the tackiest, most beautiful wedding in all of Bucks
County." She takes a sip of tea and I can see she is lost in
the memory. "Anita looked so beautiful in her vintage navy
blue suit and bow tie. Isn't she adorable?" she asks, grabbing a framed photo from the shelf behind me.

"She's something," I say, trying to reconcile the word
adorable with the Anita who puts me in my place on a regular basis.

"What about you?" she asks. "Fill me in on everything."

I tell her about college and grad school and how I made
my first million. I tell her about my penthouse and the
Mercedes S-Class I bought and keep in a garage with rent
higher than my first apartment. I tell her about first-class
flights to mind-blowing vacations like the bungalows built
over the ocean in Bali.

"Oh," she says. "I suppose that's all very impressive."
She smooths her skirts across her lap. "Tell me," she says
brightly, her tone oversignaling a shift in topics. "Who are
you reading?" She gets up and pulls a book off a nearby

shelf. "Have you gotten to this collection yet? It came out last month."

She places a thin volume on the table in front of me with a green cover and the words *Eden's Promise* across the front in gold script. "No," I say. "I haven't. I've been busy."

"What about this? It's divine. The one about the meadow is absolutely rapturous." She holds up another book just as unrecognizable as the first.

"No," I say and take a sip of tea to cover how uncomfortable I am.

"So what *are* you reading? I'm sure you discover new voices in New York all the time. The scene is so vibrant there. I should go more often. You could tell me where to go."

"No, I couldn't," I say tersely. I think Toula is surprised by my tone. She puts down the book she's holding and sits across from me. "Look, the last thing I read from cover to cover was an annual report for a chemical manufacturer. And before that it was the annual report for a competing chemical manufacturer and before that something even thicker and duller."

"Well, you're busy. I'm sure once you are out here and have more time you'll…"

I don't let her finish that sentence. "I won't. Look, I don't have any interest in wasting my time reading poetry anymore."

Her hand moves to her chest in shock. "Vinny," she says, aghast. I know she just slipped but hearing that name pisses me off.

"I told you. It's Vince."

"Yes, of course, I'm sorry but you have to understand this is quite a shock for me."

"People change." My words hint at being an accusation.

She laughs quietly and grabs the book from the table. "No, not really," she says calmly. She shelves the book quickly and returns to the chair across from me.

"I've made some shifts here and there. But I've only become more of myself. I think you'll find that I haven't changed at all. People don't change, at least not the ones I know. They evolve. There's a big difference."

She's right. It could be fifteen years ago. Me rebelling. Her calmly giving me advice, encouraging me to go deeper inside to find out what makes me tick. She is exactly the same person. But that's her. Not me.

"Well, I've changed. What other choice did I have? Was I supposed to stay the weakling? Never stand on my own two feet? Always worry about who would do what to me and when? I can't live like that. I don't want to."

"Oh, I don't think you were ever as weak as you thought you were. I understand what you're saying but you can't run from who you are. Trust me, that only leads to misery."

"No, it doesn't. I've gotten as far as I can from my old self and it's great."

She raises her teacup to her lips to take a sip while keeping her eyes locked on mine. "But you left New York to come here. You came back for a reason. I'm wondering what it was…or maybe you're waiting for the reason to make itself known." Toula still holds dear her beloved everything-happens-for-a-reason philosophy but it was always a bitter pill for me to swallow.

"I know exactly why I'm here," I say and tear my eyes away. Her gaze has a way of forcing cracks in my protective shell and I don't want to crack open any further than I already have since being here.

"It was nice seeing you," I say, moving my teacup to the side and standing up to leave. "I'm glad you're so happy. I really am. I have a lot of work to do at the inn."

I walk out the door wondering if I should have ever walked in.

Chapter Fourteen

The weekend tourist crowds are beginning to fill the streets. They wander in and out of the cottage shops and take photos of the stately Victorian mansions painted like the eyelids of baby drag queens. I cross the street to The Beautiful Things Shoppe and look at myself in the reflection of the window. The eyes that stare back at me are that of a scared teenager. I walk toward the river to see if the breeze that blows on even the stillest afternoons still has a calming effect on me.

It doesn't.

Poetry. Toula thinks I still read poetry like some lovesick teenager. I don't need poetry and books. What did any of that stuff ever get me before? Nothing but heartache.

I remember when Toula found a used copy of a book of

poetry by Barbara Guest that I had been wanting for weeks. Trees had just started getting buds but the leaves weren't out yet. It was a warm enough evening to sit by the river without a jacket so I sat on a bench and took a few seconds to stare at the river before losing myself in the poetry of "Parachutes, My Love, Could Carry Us Higher."

Suddenly the book was pulled from my hands. "I didn't know you had to read a book to learn to be a faggot."

I looked up and Mark Noonan loomed over me. He tossed the book on the ground. Mark was freakishly big for a tenth grader and he terrified me. I bent down to the ground to pick up my book and he kicked it away from me. There were a few other boys with him but I kept my head down. Sometimes kids would cross the river looking to cause trouble. New Hope was only a safe place as much as any place is really safe for queer kids. I just wanted my book so I reached for it again. And he kicked it away.

They laughed.

"You don't need a fucking book to tell you how to be a fudge packer, Skinny Vinny. You're like the faggiest faggot I've ever seen. What are you fucking wearing?"

I was wearing my usual uniform. Huge jeans that I belted with a vintage tie and a black T-shirt so big it could have fit two people inside it. I thought I was hiding my miserably skinny body. That day I was wearing just a smidge of Wet n Wild blush. Such a little amount you could barely see it. It was an experiment. I lived every minute in school with my head down, avoiding conflict, constantly scared that some gesture or mispronunciation would betray me and expose me. But here in New Hope I thought I could exercise the smallest amount of freedom.

"Holy shit. Are you wearing makeup?"

The sun was setting and I'm sure the evening shadows made it hard to make out the detail on my face but of course this asshole didn't miss anything. I looked down. From the corner of my eyes I could see other boys from school. Louis Patterson was there and Ralph Ammer. In the distance farther down on the river walk I saw another boy but he was so far away I couldn't tell who it was or if he was even with them. For a second, I thought it might be Tack but before I could get a good look Mark grabbed the book.

"You don't need this book. Go home and fix your makeup, sweetheart." He picked it up from the ground and tossed it over the railing into the Delaware River. That made everyone laugh hysterically. A small group of tourists with ice cream cones approached and it spooked Mark enough to run off with his crowd hollering and laughing hysterically like they just watched their team score a winning goal.

There was just enough light to watch the book float on the surface for a few seconds before traveling downriver to a watery grave.

Excuse me if I don't think of New Hope as a shrine to queer liberation. I don't believe the mindless mantra that community builds strength. Strength builds strength. Period. Maybe Anita and Toula aren't impressed by the things I've worked for but the rest of the world is.

The pretty streets and scenic views here might have softened me a bit at first but it's clear I made a mistake coming back. This place didn't protect me then and I don't need to protect it now. Let FunTyme Inc. turn the whole village into a parking lot for all I care. I can almost smell the hot asphalt.

Chapter Fifteen

Tack

The smell of ripe wild strawberries always reminds me of Ma. She would harvest them from the secret meadow on Hendricks Island and then chop off the stems and use a paring knife to carve them just enough so they looked like tender hearts. She'd put them in my cereal, hand me my spoon and say, "Eat your heart out." It always made me laugh.

I don't have that many memories of her because I was so young when she died but almost all of them take place in that kitchen on the farm with the window-paned white cabinets and the huge kitchen table where she made everything from beef stew to lemon meringue pie. I still have her recipes.

The kitchen in the owner's suite is not nearly as big as the one on the farm but it has everything I need to make the strawberry and goat cheese bruschetta recipe I came up with during my first semester of culinary school. I wash the strawberries, gently treating each one like a precious orchid. The freshest berries bruise easily so I take extra care to make sure the water doesn't spray too forcefully. I chop the strawberries with as sharp a knife as I can find. I make an emulsion of local honey and balsamic vinegar, then pour the sweet and tart dressing over the clean berries. I let the contrasting flavors marinate in the bowl, giving them time to draw each other out.

From the kitchen I can see into Vince's room. The jackets from his expensive suits are thrown on the bed and his pants are a wrinkled ball on the floor. Drawers are open, the closet is in shambles and the bed isn't made. Vince walks around all polished and groomed but he leaves a tornado of mess behind. The neat freak in me wants to go in there and fold every piece of clothing.

I start slicing the fresh baguette I bought at the bakery on the corner opposite the bridge and place it on the baking sheet. My eyes keep darting back to Vince's room. I could just close the door so the mess doesn't taunt me, but despite the disarray I like having this secret window into how he lives now. I'm about to spread the goat cheese on the toast when Vince walks in.

"Perfect timing," I say. "You have to try these strawberry bruschetta. They'll be a great starter on the new menu. Anita and I think we can open by the end of June. Strawberries will still be in season and we can add blueberries."

He stands in the doorway, his wide frame filling it like a statue in an archway at a museum. He does not look like he had a relaxing stroll around town. He looks like he just came back from a post office in hell.

"Next week," he says firmly.

I use an offset spatula to spread the smooth goat cheese over the rough surface of the toasted bread. "The blueberries won't be ripe by next week," I say. "I saw some over in Point Pleasant. They're getting big but still more greenish-violet than deep blue."

"Not the berries," Vince says, moving into the living room. "Us."

Us? The word startles me and Vince immediately corrects himself. "Not *us*. This place. The Hideaway Inn. It opens for dinner. Next week."

Anita and I spent all morning figuring out suppliers and menus and when certain crops would be ready. Setting up the kitchen for dinner service alone will take two weeks and getting the supplies will take longer. "You're joking."

"I'm not. We open next week." It's clear this is not up for discussion.

"There is no way we can get the food and dry goods we need by then. It's not possible. Half the items on the menu aren't even ripe yet."

"Give me the menu. I still have contacts in New York. I can get what you need. We'll get frozen if we have to. You cook it. That's all you have to do, Tack. Cook."

He is on the opposite side of the counter from me. What happened this afternoon to make him return in such a mood? I know I should be annoyed but I can't help looking at how his dark scruff makes his eyes even more penetrating. I always thought he could see right through me with those deep coffee bean eyes that saw so much more than everybody else.

"Tack, are you listening to me?" He knocks on the kitchen counter just next to my bowl of berries. His tone is less aggressive but still unwavering. "We have to open next week. I'll get what you need. I can't afford to stay closed."

I'm about to go into more detail about the seasonal bruschetta I made for him when he grabs a few pieces of toast that haven't been finished with berries, stacks them together, and puts them in his mouth like he's eating a hoagie. He goes to his room and closes the door behind him.

Next week? That seems absolutely impossible. I know the menu I created is good. I don't have a single doubt the food will be delicious. But I need more time. I know he has a stubborn streak but I don't remember all this anger.

"It's just Vinny," I whisper to myself. He would lose it if he heard me from the other side of his door.

I spoon the strawberry mixture over the remaining toasts. No sense wasting all these delicious ingredients. These will make a fantastic lunch. I take out a small plate and pour myself a glass of water. By now Vince's bed is probably covered in crumbs from the toast and he has goat cheese all over his thick fingers.

Who would have thought this kid would have turned out to be such a hard-ass? He thinks he's this big tough guy now and maybe he is. That doesn't mean he still isn't the kid I knew at the fence. He could have purchased an inn anywhere along the Delaware, anywhere in the world from the way he talks about his wealth. But he chose right here in New Hope. He wouldn't move back here if there wasn't a reason and after seeing how he uses that stuck open bathroom door like a personal peep show maybe part of the reason is finishing what we started.

When Vince first approached me about working here I thought that I would finally show him that I've matured. That I'm no longer a hundred steps behind him. But just when I thought I'd caught up he has gone in a different direction. I didn't have the courage to catch up to him when we were in high school but this time I'm not going to let him get away so easily.

I take a bite of my creation and the strawberries gently release their sweet juice with each bite but the vinegar is a little overpowering. Next time I'll use more honey to get the result I want.

Chapter Sixteen

A week later, I wake up to the smell of pancakes creeping under my bedroom door. It would be easier to ignore an ambulance siren. I keep putting my pillow over my face but eventually I have to follow my nose. I open the bedroom door and find Tack in the small kitchen standing behind the stove wearing a pair of tiny running shorts, a tank top and an apron. He looks like a hot combination of Olympic medalist and short-order cook.

"Good morning," he says, lifting a pancake off the griddle and onto a plate with a spatula. I'm about to imagine what it would be like if I ripped off that apron but I stop myself. The only way to deal with this is to shut the feelings off completely. I knew having him move in here with me would be a problem; I just never thought I'd have to wear a gas mask to resist him.

"I'm experimenting with a coconut coulis that I think will offset the tartness of the blueberries nicely." He hands me a plate with fluffy golden discs dotted with berries and a porcelain teacup filled with a creamy white sauce. It looks amazing but I raise my eyebrows and give him a look before taking the plate and sitting at the table near the window that overlooks the river.

"Is something wrong?" he asks.

"No. It's just that hearing words like *coconut coulis* come out of your mouth still takes some getting used to." I take my fork and stab into the cakes. The balance of the two flavors is perfect and I can't hide the reaction on my face.

"So you like the sauce?" he asks with a sly confidence that is as sexy as his almost-naked torso in an apron.

"Sauce. Now that sounds more like Tack," I say, turning back to him and swallowing the incredible confection. A smile creeps across my face despite my best effort. "You used to put ketchup on the school cafeteria pizza." I still wince at the thought of it.

Tack laughs, which somehow makes the pancakes taste even better. I'd forgotten the power of his laugh. The sound of it could wake me out of an awful mood. "I still love ketchup."

"I remember those disgusting ketchup sandwiches you would bring with you to work on the fence." As soon as the words come out, I catch myself. I've been thinking about the past and that summer but I don't want him to know that.

"So you do remember that summer?" He walks over to me and places his hand on my shoulder. The skin to skin contact creates an electric network of feelings and desire that speeds across my brain and body like a supercomputer rebooting.

For a moment we are back in the field. Two boys figuring out who they are and what they want. I'm about to dive back into those golden, sun-dappled memories but I squeeze the thoughts out of my brain. I won't let him take me off course. I won't get pulled in by his magnetic force again.

I shake my head to release the thought and jerk my shoulder out from under his hand as I stand up, grabbing my plate. I take the uneaten food and dump it into the trash before changing the subject. The quick frown that appears on Tack's face shows me his disappointment. I change the subject.

"Tack, I'm focused on *this* summer and you should be too. We open tonight. Did you get an update on the steaks?"

I go back to the table and open my laptop, using the screen like a shield from him. Still, I get the feeling he can't make sense of the kid he once knew, who couldn't get enough of him, and the man who now keeps pushing him away. Even I don't completely understand who I am in this moment. The one thing I do understand is that the restaurant is opening tonight and we have advertised a New York Steak Night Special to get people in the door and we have no steaks. My panic was diminished by the sweet smell of buttery pancakes but it suddenly hits me like a sack of day-old biscuits.

"No update," he says and busies himself putting away the dishes.

"Did you call Cheryl?"

"Of course. I left another message."

Cheryl has contacts at a high-end butcher in Brooklyn and said she could get me a great price on some dry-aged steaks. As soon as I made the order, though, her brother-in-law fell off a ladder and she's been missing in action. Her assistant keeps assuring us the steaks will be here.

"We need those steaks," I mutter. I'm planning to use them as a loss leader to get people in the door.

"Did you call the guys at Haring Brothers Meats as a backup? They're less than ten miles away but they need at least two days."

Haring Brothers? I've been so stressed about connecting with Cheryl that I totally forgot to place the backup order with Haring Brothers. How could I make such a screwup? Then I take a look at Tack's sleeveless arms and the apron strapped across his tight body and I realize that between shower shows and impromptu tastings, I've been distracted. Still, it's my fault.

"I said I'd take care of it." The words squeak out of my mouth. I can't tell him I forgot.

"But did you?" he asks.

"I've had a lot on my mind this week. And we won't need an extra order of steaks when the ones from New York get here." I dodge the question because I don't want to let him see my error. It's not just pride. After all my going on about my business acumen I don't want him to think I'm incompetent.

I can't tell if he sees through me or not. He puts his hand on my arm and says, "Vince, we need to have a backup plan." His hand on the skin of my forearm feels more comforting than electric in this moment but still I recoil. I can't open that door.

"You know what we could do?" he asks and his use of the first person plural makes my head fuzzy again. "I have this recipe for these amazing bean burgers. I use three kinds of beans and this creamy goat cheese from down the road with fresh parsley."

"*Bean* burgers?" I ask him like he suggested we serve apple juice and Oreos.

"Yeah, why not?" he asks, brushing his bangs off his forehead and casually shrugging his shoulders.

"Because we have a page of reservations for Steak Night. Not Bean Night." The thing I used to love about Tack is also the thing that drives me nuts. He thinks of the world as a place that will just play along with him. His considerable charm and indisputable good looks have helped him pave a path free of thorns and dead ends. I live in reality and have spent my life scratching and fighting for the things I want.

"If we dress them up a bit and serve some seasonal veggies, I think people would love them."

I shake my head. "That's the stupidest thing I've ever heard."

It takes me a second to realize what I said. I should not have used the word *stupid*, not to Tack. He was never a great student and self-conscious about it. "I'm sorry," I say but it's hard for me to go any further than that. I should let my guard down. I should admit that I didn't call Haring Brothers so that tonight doesn't turn into a total disaster. I have a feeling he would be understanding—he knows how much stress I've been under. But I'm not ready to show him my faults or accept his understanding. I'm not sure I'll ever be. "Tack, I know you have food to prep. I'll be in my room working on my meat." I walk straight to my bedroom but catch a glimpse of his bewildered face before shutting the door behind me.

I'll be working on my meat? I hold my hands to my face like the Munch painting and let out a silent scream. I'm sure Tack is getting a good laugh over my very poor choice of words. It feels exactly like when we were kids, with me saying stupid things that I analyze over and over again once I'm alone. I have to pull myself together.

A few hours before we open, after Cheryl's assistant has confirmed multiple times that the steaks are on their way, I get dressed for the big opening. I put on my most expensive three-piece blue linen suit I had custom made in Milan and give myself one last look in the mirror before I hear Tack coming into the apartment. I walk out hoping to hear good news.

He's in his chef gear, all gleaming white. When he sees me, he stops. "Wow, you look great, Vince. Very handsome." For just a second there is no impending doom. There is just this very attractive man noticing me in the middle of the apartment we happen to share. Before I can let my fantasy go any further he interrupts my thoughts with an update. "I have news about the steaks."

"Please tell me they are in New Hope this very minute," I ask, his compliment fluttering out of my mind.

"As a matter of fact," he says, "they are." He gives me a big smile.

"That's great news. Go down and start seasoning them or whatever you need to do to make them fantastic."

"Well, I can't exactly do that." His smile drops.

"Tack, this is not the time for one of your riddles. I thought you said they're in New Hope."

"They are. Unfortunately, they're in New Hope, New York. About four hours away from here."

I can almost feel the veins popping out of my forehead. "What? You've got to be kidding me." This isn't just about having a successful opening. It's about proving myself. It's about showing Tack that I've made something of myself, that I've become a man worthy of his… I stop myself from finishing the thought.

"A simple GPS mistake. Is there an order we can maybe send someone to Haring Brothers for if…"

"That's not going to happen." If he hasn't already figured out I didn't place the order he certainly has now. This is a complete disaster. Why didn't I just admit to him that I forgot? Then at least I would have been able to come up with some options. I don't want Tack to see that I'm in a panic so I go cold and steely on him. "Look, you just worry about cooking. That's what you're here to do. I'll figure out something."

"Can't we work together on this?"

"You're the chef. I'm the owner. You worry about what

happens in the kitchen once the food is here. I worry about everything else."

"I know you're stressed. I get that, but I'm on your side." He looks at me plainly with his eyes focused on mine. Then he adds a bit more gently, "I always have been."

I quickly tilt my head down and cover my forehead and eyes with my hand to give the appearance I'm thinking through some ideas. I just can't look at him in this moment. I can't even be in the same room. "Just go," I order. "I'll be downstairs in a minute."

I watch his feet move to the door and out the apartment. As soon as I'm sure he is out of earshot I slam my fist against the wall. I have a dining room about to be filled with customers expecting steak dinners and an investment that is about to go belly-up but the thing that has me most upset is letting Tack see me fail. What does he even mean with this I've-always-been-on-your-side stuff? Every time I think about going downstairs to find a solution with Tack I also think about his hand on my arm and how safe it made me feel before I brushed it off. The more I connect with him, the more I let down my defenses and I'd rather jump in the river with my suit on than do that.

If I can't be honest with myself, at least I can be honest with the customers, or rather, future former customers. Just before we are scheduled to open the doors, I head downstairs. I'm about to walk through the kitchen to the front entrance dining room when I hear Anita and Tack talking about the steaks on the other side of the dining room door. I hang back and eavesdrop.

"New Hope, New York?" I hear Anita ask. She is almost

shouting. "Can we send someone to pick up the Haring Brothers order? We can delay a bit."

"There is no order at Haring Brothers," Tack says to her.

"Did he think he was too good for a local butcher? Had to have his fancy New York steaks from some hipster butcher shop." It's hard to be mad at Anita when this whole thing is my fault.

I'm about to open the door when I hear Tack say: "No, it wasn't him. It was me. I forgot to call. Don't blame him. It's my fault."

What? This was his opportunity to save his reputation and expose me to her as a phony and he didn't take it. Could it be that Tack really is on my side?

I catch a glimpse of my watch and realize it's almost time to open. I walk out the back and around to the street entrance of the inn so Tack and Anita don't realize I've overheard them. A small group of people is waiting on the sidewalk, under the sign Anita made: "NY Strip Steak Special—One Night Only."

"Thanks for coming," I say brightly, putting a Band-Aid on my own disappointment. "I'm Vince Amato, the new owner of The Hideaway Inn. I'm afraid the steaks had a bit of trouble getting here tonight." There is a grumbling of dissatisfaction. I smile sheepishly, trying to make the best of it. "But we still have some great things on the menu." What exactly I don't know. I wish now I hadn't been so quick to dismiss those bean burgers.

Tack appears out the front door and is greeted by a few people who know him. He smiles and shakes hands like he's running for office. "Sorry about any confusion, everyone. You know what they say, you can lead a horse to water but you can't get a steak over the river."

They laugh at his joke and even though it's lame, I laugh too.

"The owner will give anyone who wishes a rain check to come back later in the summer once we have those steaks. Tonight, I'm serving my bean burgers for anybody who wants to give us a try. I promise—once you try my veggie burgers, you might never want a steak again." Tack pats me on the shoulder to emphasize his point and he leaves his hand there just long enough for me to connect with his touch. This time I don't recoil. I let the feeling of his hand on my body linger until he moves it to open the door of the inn and let customers through.

He welcomes each guest and I help the people who ask for rain checks. Once the last patron is inside, we are alone on the sidewalk. "Not the opening you were planning but we have a few people in there. I better go cook up those bean burgers."

"You mean the bean burgers I stubbornly told you not to make?"

"Exactly. Aren't you glad I suck at being told what to do?"

Why is he so determined to help me? Sure, he wants to protect the reputation of the inn and his cooking but telling Anita it was his fault is beyond anything professional. It feels like more than that. Could he still have feelings for me? *Still* is not the right word. I'm not sure he ever did. I'm so confused.

"Thank you," I say with a wide smile that I don't stop from spreading across my face.

"You're welcome," Tack says with a smile as wide as my own. Our eyes meet for just a few seconds but it's enough to feel that connection.

Tack walks into The Hideaway and my willpower for resisting him fades like the sun setting over the Delaware.

Chapter Seventeen

Tack

"Get in," I tell Vince, holding open the truck door. I've
even brushed off some of the hay that usually clings to the
seats in the cab.

Vince has just come out of the inn. He's wearing a tight
tank top that shows off his arms and scoops low enough
to reveal a tangle of dark hair on his upper chest. His basketball shorts and sneakers that look more expensive than
my truck make me think he is headed to the gym but the
extra-dark sunglasses and unshaven face indicate he might
just be trying to escape last night's disaster.

He looks at me over his shades. "I'm not exactly in the

mood to have my spleen shaken out of me as your hunk of junk avoids the maze of potholes in this town."

I clap my hands over the side view mirror and whisper, "Don't listen to him, Axel. He doesn't mean it." I pat my truck gently. "I'm going to overlook your ugly comments because I know last night was a bit rough."

"A bit rough? I've seen cage matches that went more smoothly than last night. I got a text this morning that the delivery truck is now somewhere in Canada."

"That's exactly what this trip is going to solve. I want you to meet Paul."

"Who is Paul and why do I want to meet him?"

I smile and push my bangs off my forehead. I'm not above using some of my obvious appeal to get Vince to do what I want. I've never been the kind of guy to really lean into the whole charm thing but then again I never thought I'd have a second chance with Vince. Now that he's finally had a bit of a comeuppance maybe I can get him to take down his shield for a few moments. Last night was a disaster and we both know it. I want to show him that I know what I'm talking about when it comes to food. I know he wants to be seen for who he is now and so do I.

"Get in the truck and you'll find out," I say, making sure my grin is devilish as can be.

"Fine," he says and gets in the truck.

I turn down Main Street and instead of crossing the river I take the road west, deeper into the Pennsylvania farmlands that surround the area. Once we get past the ridge that runs along the Delaware, the land flattens out and the landscape is a mix of wealthy weekender estates and old farms still making a go of it. Strict and aggressive land preservation has limited a good deal of new construction so the rural nature of the community is still strong. We head down one of my favorite roads. It has so many peaks and valleys it feels like we're on a kiddie coaster at the shore.

"Roll down your window," I tell Vince once we are a few miles down the road. I keep one arm on the wheel and use the other to quickly roll down mine.

"I'm fine..." he starts to say and then I see a glimmer of recognition in his eye. "Oh, right. It's just up here. Is it still there?"

"Roll down your window and you tell me."

He rolls down his window and wind fills the cab. At first it's just air and then the wind magically transforms to purple, blue and indigo swirls that twirl around us like bolts of energy. I take a deep breath and the calming lavender scent fills my lungs.

"Wow. That smell is still so strong," he says. He closes his eyes to take a deep breath, and I steal a deeper glance at him without his knowing. I catch a glimpse underneath his mask and it's beautiful, although hard to see for very long.

He opens his eyes and I make sure I'm looking straight ahead on the road. "There it is," I say, pointing to the side of the road, "Langford Lavender Farm." A faded hand-painted sign with purple flowers hangs off a rickety wooden post. Pale knee-high bushes with purple tops just beginning to emerge dot the open landscape.

"I can't believe it's still here," he says, shaking his head.

"Why?"

"I don't know. It's like I moved away and this place is trapped in a time warp."

"No one gets trapped in a place as beautiful as this," I tell him plainly. I don't like what he's implying. I want him to remember how extraordinary this area is. He is so focused on making the inn a success that I can't reach him in the way I want to. Not really. I figure a little sensory overload might help melt the ice.

"A canary in the most beautifully gilded cage is still in a cage," he retorts, all winter and chill.

"I do not live in a cage," I say, unable to hide the fact that now he is pissing me off.

"Of course you don't," he says, but I can tell he is just paying me lip service. "But look at Langford Farm. I mean, lavender as a crop? Seriously? What can the profit margin be on that? Now, soybeans have an established market. Soybeans could make a nice profit, I'm sure."

"Yeah," I say, hiding my anger behind sarcasm. "Wouldn't it be great to drive down here and smell the soybeans? Not everything is about profit, you know." I roll up my window quicker than I rolled it down. Maybe I just can't get through to the Vince I want to see again.

He lets out a combination snort-laugh and says, "Sure." His sarcasm tops mine by ten. "People say that, but when you shake it down money means something. It makes people pay attention. It makes them do what you want."

"Your family was poorer than mine. Your mom worked two jobs just to make ends meet. She left for the diner before dawn and didn't get home until after the gas station closed. You hated that."

Vince rolls up his window and stares out blankly. I shouldn't have mentioned his mother. She passed away a few years after we graduated high school, when Vince would have still been in college. His mother was the only family he had, since his dad had run off while she was pregnant with him. "It must be hard to be back here and not have her around," I say as gently as I can.

"It's fine," he says without emotion.

"Everybody liked your mom," I say. She served eggs and pumped gas with the same friendly smile. If you ate or drove, it was hard not to know her.

"I know."

"I'm sorry," I say.

"For what?"

Now that's a hard question. For your mom dying. For letting you down. For not loving you back. I decide to go with the easiest of the three—and it's not lost on me that confronting the death of his mom is suddenly the easiest option. I wanted to say goodbye to his mom when I heard that she had passed so suddenly but Vince made it impossible. He didn't have any type of memorial service. Still, I should have tried harder to pay my respects, to let him know I cared.

"For not reaching out," I say, hoping that covered multiple options. I keep my hands on the wheel and focus on the road. The scent of lavender slowly evaporates, taking the carefree moment with it as the mood becomes somber. Vince turns his head to look out the passenger window.

What do I do now? Would it be too weird to grab his hand to let him know how much I cared about him, that

I still care about him? I glance down and see his hand on the seat of the truck. It would be so easy to just hold it right now. It would let him know so much of what I want to tell him beyond the restaurant, beyond New Hope, beyond everything.

"Thank you," he says quietly, the breath barely leaving his mouth. "It's nice to hear that. And nice to remember that everyone liked her."

We hit a bump in the road. The truck rocks up and down and bangs Vince's head against the roof. It cracks me up to see how pissed off he gets every time he hits his head so I aim for the potholes like I'm playing a video game.

A line of massive ash trees creates a canopy over the driveway to the farm. I pull over to a patch of field just a few yards from the largest barn on the property. I hop out of the truck and smile at Vince, thinking about our conversation and how close it made me feel to him. I just needed to know that we could still do it. We can still connect at that deep emotional level even though he fights against it.

My eyes catch his for just a moment and then his quickly dart away. We'll get there. We just need the right moment.

Chapter Eighteen

The estate Tack's brought me to is beautiful and clearly not a weekender's country house. The mud-covered tractors, well-worn tracks to the open fields and smell of manure make it clear that this is a working agricultural space, but the main residence is right out of a real estate brochure: vintage stonework that will last at least another century and white clapboard with just the exact amount of paint peeling to make it look rustic.

A scraggly brown and white goat runs over to Tack like a kid going after a second slice of birthday cake. The goat lets out a loud bleat.

Tack puts his hand on the goat's neck and gently pats. "This is Paul," he says.

"This is a goat," I say plainly and maybe with a hint of

incredulity. "You brought me all the way out here on a hot morning to meet a goat?"

The goat bleats even louder this time.

"Paul thinks he's my boyfriend." Tack takes a carrot out of his pocket. The goat—Paul, rather—licks his fingers and then inhales the carrot in one single gulp. Paul would be very popular at The Eagle on Dollar Beer Night.

But I see an opening. I'm tired of tiptoeing around Tack's sexuality. I spent most of my young adult life guessing *is he or isn't he*. Was it all in my head or did he feel the same things I was feeling? When he married Evie I thought the book was slammed closed but it seems like that book has been taken off the shelf and opened. It's time to find out who is what.

"So, you have boyfriends now?" I ask as casually as possible. I lean over the fence as if I couldn't care less about the answer. I could have asked him about the weather or the gross national debt or directions to the closest Staples. I pet the other side of Paul's neck so I have something to do with my hands.

"Not really," he says, just as casually as I asked. I turn my head and can't help but roll my eyes. Is that how he is going to play it?

"Oh," I say, my tone frigid.

"I mean I'm bi. I could have a boyfriend," he says, catching my eye and hanging there for just a moment longer than he should. "I just don't have a boyfriend right now."

Vinny would have asked a hundred questions and tried to have gotten Tack to open up but I don't do that anymore. I don't let my emotions get the better of me. I won't let Tack have power over me. The steelier silent I am the more power I have. I breathe in and out staring straight ahead. Not a word. Until there are all the words.

"So you're bi. I didn't know that. I mean, I knew you married Evie and then broke up but I wasn't sure if you were into guys. I thought you might be gay because, well, but… I didn't want to assume and I didn't want to ask although I guess I just did. So, you're bi."

I slap my hand to my mouth like I am brushing something off my face but really, I am holding my big trap shut. So much for my polished study in controlled masculinity.

"Yeah, I'm bi," Tack says. "Obviously it took me a while to confront those feelings with any maturity. But I'm out. Everyone knows."

"Even your dad?" I ask, squinting my eyes, afraid of the reply.

"Even him. I don't think he'll be starting a PFLAG chapter anytime soon but he knows."

Wow. That's really incredible news. I want to run over to him and hug him and celebrate and tell him how proud I am but I don't even let a trace of that emotion reach the surface.

"Is that why you and Evie broke up?" I figure if I ask one question instead of a parade of interrogative statements I'll be able to maintain my composure.

"Partly, maybe. Not really. I don't know. Things with Evie never really worked that way and I think we both knew it. We tried, but once we were married things got even harder. It wasn't just confronting my sexuality. It was more about confronting my identity. Evie was on her own path too. But people expected me to do certain things and act a certain way and it was so much easier to meet everyone's expectations."

The goat bleats again and Tack soothes the animal by petting him on the top of the nose.

"I can understand that." I think of walking into a real estate closing and how important it is for me to dress a certain way and perform this "master of the universe" routine for everyone. It's easier to play the part people expect you to play.

"I'm surprised you understand," Tack says quietly.

"Surprised I understand? What do you mean?"

"In school you didn't exactly meet people's expectations. You always did your own thing."

My own thing? That isn't exactly how I would think of it. Mostly I was invisible and the times I wasn't, I was considered a complete freak or weirdo. The only time I felt normal was when I was with him that summer. With him I felt like it was okay to just be myself. At least I felt that way until it was clear he didn't want anything to do with me. The rejection was hard and it made me not want anything to do with me either. I thought poetry and makeup experiments were part of the reason he rejected me. How could he be with someone who was the object of so much ridicule?

"Vince, I don't think you have any idea how much I looked up to you in high school."

I am solid stone, completely—not because I am performing my hyper-masculine emotionless robot but because I am so shocked by what Tack has just said.

"For what?" I ask, thinking back to the way I felt so small and unimportant as I walked down the hall, hoping no one would notice me and shove me in the shoulder.

"Are you serious?" Tack asks. He truly has no idea what I'm asking.

"I want to know what exactly you looked up to back then. The way I was teased by your friends every time I walked anywhere near the boys' locker room? Or maybe you looked up to me from the other side of the locker I was pushed into? Or when…"

"All right, I get it. Enough. I was trying to pay you a compliment. I can't do anything right around you anymore. I feel like shit for what happened to you. How you were treated."

He still doesn't get it. I don't care about how I was treated. That isn't the wound that's still tender. It's his role on the sidelines that still kills me.

I take a pause from the argument to gather my thoughts. The sun is climbing in the sky and I can feel the sting of its rays on my neck as I try to think of a way to show him what I mean. "Do you remember where you were when I was getting teased and harassed?"

"I don't know. At the farm working?"

Paul must feel the intensity of our conversation since he slowly walks away, leaving us alone by the fence.

"Sometimes," I say. "But a lot of times you were right there."

Tack can't look at me. He darts his eyes to the side. "I never teased you. Not once. I never called you names."

He is defiant at the very thought that I would accuse him of harassing me.

"No," I say. "Of course you didn't. I know that." I try to get the conversation to a more reasonable tone so I can make my point. "Look, you remember the day that Mark Noonan pushed me into the locker because I wore eye-liner to school?" Another makeup experiment I immediately regretted.

"Yes," he says and I see a tiny smile on the edge of his lips.

"This is a good memory for you?" I ask sharply. The hint of a smile instantly disappears.

"No, of course not. I was thinking of how cute you looked in your eyeliner. Like a rock star. I'm wondering if you still wear it."

"Never," I say flatly. As if I would go to an acquisitions meeting dressed like Elton John. He sees me now and he must see how ridiculous that question is. "Don't change the subject. You remember Mark doing that."

"Yes, I do," he says solemnly.

"Did you read my diary to have that memory or did I tell you about it?"

"No, of course not," he says.

"So you remember because you were there. You and Mark were friends, for fuck's sake."

"We weren't friends," he snaps back.

"Tack, get off it. You were on the same teams. You both played football and ran track. You went to parties at his house with Evie all the time."

"But I…" He trails off. His soft eyes look tense and his

lower lip covers his upper lip. A calm silence fills the pasture and I look away. I can hear goats playing on the other side of the pen and a tractor growls farther in the distance. The acid smell of fertilizer cuts across my nostrils. I turn back to look at Tack. His face is twisted and his eyes are tense. My first reaction is to comfort him. I don't like seeing him so upset but I also know I need him to face the truth. I can't work with him and live with him without him knowing that his act of complicity created the deepest cut.

"I know," he says, looking right in my eyes. "I should have said something. I should have stopped it but I didn't. I stood there and let it happen time and time again. I'd see you at school and avoid you. I told myself it was the best thing to do. I thought if I just kept my head down... You have no idea how many times I would make those guys walk a route that would not put you in harm's way or distract them or redirect their stupid aggression. But I didn't stop it when it was happening and there is no excuse for what I did—or what I didn't do." A tear falls out of Tack's eye and runs down his hot red cheek. I don't know if the tear is for him or me or for the us that once was and can't be again. He wipes another potential tear from his eyes and stands face to face with me.

"Vince, I'm sorry. I'm sorry for what happened to you and I'm even more sorry that I didn't stop it."

Just hearing those words and knowing he understands what he's sorry for makes something inside me collapse. One of the many walls I have built crumbles to the ground.

"Thank you," I say simply, honestly and quietly.

"I'm truly sorry. And there is something I want you to

know. Something that's important for you to know," Tack says, and then I notice his hand moving toward mine.

"Tack O'Leary, you handsome stud of a man, flirting with my goats! What are you doing here?" A tall muscular man with a bald head and a smile bigger than the pasture comes out of the barn behind the goat shelter. His boots leave behind deep footprints and the goats follow him like he is a god. He does have the body of Hercules though, all thick muscle like he was once a body builder.

I want to yell, "Go back. Go back! Can't you see we are having a moment!" But this guy is a human bowling ball. There is no stopping him.

"What? What did you want to tell me?" I ask Tack quickly while the guy is still far enough away that he won't be able to hear my intimate tones.

"Vince, I want you to know that…" He pauses for a second before saying, "Evie and I, we have a child. A six-year-old. An amazing six-year-old."

Chapter Nineteen

My mouth drops open at Tack's confession, and I wonder if it's medically sound for my eyes to pop out of my skull as far as they are.

"And who is the handsome specimen you brought with you?" the man walking over asks as soon as he is in front of us.

How can I shift gears like this? A six-year-old? How did that happen? I mean, I know how but it's not that which has me so stunned, it's knowing that Tack is a dad. I've been willing to expand the hot-farmer box I have him in to possibly include talented chef, but dad? My box is beginning to bust and I have about a thousand questions but I can't ask any of them in front of a stranger. Once again, Tack's timing completely sucks.

"Kevin, this is Vince Amato. Vince, this is Kevin."

Kevin stops in his tracks and pulls off his sunglasses in a dramatic sweep of his hand. "This is the famous Vince Amato. He's even more delicious-looking than you described. Those eyes. And darling, I'm going to require that you wear that tank top every time you come to visit the farm here. I do hope it's not cutting off your circulation." He shrugs. "Even if it is, I still demand that wardrobe."

I did put on one of my tightest tank tops and I know the scoop neck shows off my thick chest hair. With Kevin's mention I notice Tack's eyes drop a bit to take in my body. I'd remind him that my eyes are up top but I don't mind him checking me out at all.

"Kevin, you promised you wouldn't embarrass me," Tack says through slightly clenched teeth.

Kevin waves him away with his hand. "I promised no such thing. Anyway, it's much too late for that." Then he turns to me. "Don't worry about me. I'm perfectly harmless and happily married to the man of my dreams."

"Where is Evan?" Tack asks.

Evan and Kevin? Couples with rhyming names really need to rethink their life choices.

"He's dropping off some eggs at The Black Bass Hotel. They had a run on omelets this morning and needed more. He'll be back soon."

"That's exactly why we're here. Vince, Kevin is the man who is going to make sure last night's disaster never happens again."

I cannot let the disaster from last night repeat itself. I

have to block out the bombshell Tack just dropped and focus on business at least until we are alone again.

Kevin opens the paddock and steps outside of the gate between us. His physical presence does something to shift the intense energy and help Tack and me reset. We move from lingering feelings about the past to both being concerned about the present.

"Kevin and his husband Evan run this place. Chickens and goats, all humanely raised, all organic and all local. The goat cheese is known for being some of the best in the region," Tack says, looking at me.

"Sounds expensive," I say, as my transformation from heartsick to puppy to sharp business wolf completes.

"Oh, a number cruncher," Kevin says. "I get that. Evan was a hedge manager of a private firm and I worked at Goldman."

"Goldman? Impressive."

"Well, thank you for the compliment but I'm not sure how useful my degree from Morehouse in economics is when I've got my hand under a chicken's ass. Still, I love it out here."

"Why would you give all that up to come out here? It's beautiful but…" I can hear a bit too much surprise and disappointment in my voice. All I want to do is get back to that world. I want to get as far away from this place and Tack and his kid and all these complicated feelings as fast as I can.

"Uh-oh," Kevin says. "This one is tightly wound. I can see that. Let's take a walk around the farm and maybe some peace and calm will rub off on you. We'll see what

Chickira and Hennifer Lopez are up to." He walks past the gate and starts down a shady path that leads down a grass-covered hill.

"What happened to Lindsay LoHen?" Tack asks.

"So sad," Kevin says, sighing. "She ran off with Jamie the Fox."

The rest of the morning is a relaxing tour of Kevin and Evan's beautiful farm. The estate is a sprawling network of open pastures, shady retreats and stone and clapboard out-buildings gathered along a spring-fed stream that "twists and turns over stones on its way," as it were. We see goats and chickens but also a few fields of fresh herbs and even an orchard of blueberry bushes laden with huge purple-green berries that should turn blue by the beginning of July.

Kevin explains that he and his husband rebuilt the entire operation. They bought the place at auction and it needed a massive amount of work since the estate had been left abandoned for over a decade. In the kitchen near the dairy he lets me sample the goat cheese made on the farm. Tack spreads some on a cracker for me and tops it with some fresh chives and oregano. There is a creamy explosion of sharpness and comfort in my mouth and I think the cheese is only partially to blame.

The late June humidity begins to rise enough by early afternoon that the crisp air turns heavy. Kevin takes us out of the kitchen and down the stone path closer to the stream. "This way," he says, holding up the low branches of a majestic willow tree.

Behind the tree is an oasis. A lush stream bends around a

smooth jetty of rock and the turn forces the water to gurgle as it passes by. Ferns dot the far side of the stream and a cluster of trees create a canopy that filters the sunlight so that the leaves shimmer like emerald stained glass.

Kevin sits down on a rock and takes off his shoes and socks then rolls up his pant legs before dipping his feet into the water. Tack and I start to do the same.

Kevin takes a loud breath in and out and then gazes across the stream to the forest. "Shinrin-yoku," he says as he tilts his head back to soak it all in.

"Is that the name of those trees?" I ask.

"No," he says, taking another breath. "It's the reason we left finance to come out here. Shinrin-yoku is a Japanese word. It doesn't have an English equivalent. It basically means forest-bathing. It's considered a way of healing and Evan needed that. Well, really we both needed that after the pressure of the city."

Kevin's cell phone dings. "Speaking of Evan," he says, looking at the screen. "Hmm. Hard to believe there is such a thing as a cheese emergency but Evan has just texted to assure me that there is." Kevin pulls his feet out of the water.

I go to get up and Kevin stops me. "Don't let my cheese emergency interrupt you. Stay. Enjoy the trees. A pleasure to meet you, Vince. You've seen the operation. You've tasted the product. If you think any of our goods are the right fit for your restaurant, Evan would be happy to talk numbers when he returns." He puts on his shoes as we finish taking off ours. He pushes back the branches to exit but before he leaves, he turns. "By the way, the creek is deep enough here for a swim if you two want to go skinny-dipping. With me and Evan it's more of a chunky dunk but you get the idea." He chuckles to himself over his joke, delighted that he has given the pot one last stir.

I look at Tack and he looks back at me. The air is sticky and thick by our heads but our feet dangle just above the cool rushing water and I can feel the cold on the bottoms of my feet.

"Are you ready?" Tack asks. I'm not at all but I nod and we both put our feet in the water at the same time. We feel the icy sensation of the water in the same moment. I stifle a sharp yelp and just let the freezing water cool me down and I see the grimace on Tack's face. We are sharing the experience. No one is swooping in to save the day, no one is in charge. We're just together, for a moment, in the woods.

The water creates an uncontrollable sensation. I want to pull my feet out but I fight against the urge and I'm rewarded when the initial shock gives way to the relaxing calm of the cool water. I let my defenses down and close my eyes and try to just be on the side of this beautiful creek with this canopy of green and with Tack. Shinrin-yoku.

"This feels great," he says quietly.

"Agreed," I mutter back, rolling my head back and stirring the water with my toes.

My defenses are down so I can't hold back what's on my mind.

"Tell me about your kid," I say casually. I'm genuinely curious.

"Sure," Tack says. "What do you want to know?"

"Well, is it a boy or a girl?" I ask, my feet still pulling me into a state of relaxation.

"That's a hard question to answer," he says. I open my eyes and look over at him. His mood has not seemed to shift at all.

"Oh," I say, realizing the question I thought was the easiest might be the hardest. His eyes are still closed as his face stretches up to meet a beam of sunlight that has found its way through the leaves. When he opens them I turn away, but not as quickly as I might have yesterday.

"Jules is a wonderful kid. Always has been. Pure joy, happiness and imagination. When they were born we named them James."

"After your uncle?" Tack always thought his uncle James was a god. Tack's mom died in a car accident and James was the only connection Tack had to that side of the family.

"Exactly."

"But you call him Jules."

"I call them Jules," Tack says with a mild correction. "Jules is the bravest person I've ever met." He looks at me quickly and corrects himself: "One of the bravest people I have ever met. They have always loved dresses and tea parties and dancing but also trucks and physical activity. But whenever they would ask their kindergarten teacher at school if they could play with a doll or dance in a tutu, the teacher would force them to start throwing a football or some other hyper-masculine bullshit."

I look down at the water with a severe pang of guilt. My entire life is hyper-masculine bullshit now. I know what it's like to be told you have to act a certain way. My response was to shut down, readjust, conform.

"So you think Jules is trans?" I ask.

"They are six. I don't know. I mean, maybe. I mean, I don't know. They don't like being forced into some boy things but they love trucks. I don't think they understand themselves as a girl but they like to wear dresses. Or maybe they do. I don't know. They like being called Jules and Jules likes being called they so we do that." Tack takes a rock from his side and throws it into the stream. "All I know is that I'm not going to force him to be something he isn't. He's my kid and I love them and they can be whatever the fuck he wants to be. I don't want him to feel he has to be anything. I don't want him to feel they have to be trans or that they aren't allowed to be."

I notice his pronouns slide but I'm very conscious of his effort.

"It's just hard. We were talking about the past and I wanted you to know because I always regretted how I behaved but now, with Jules, it's more than regret I have. I won't make the same mistakes I made not standing up for you. When I see Jules being stifled I remember how you were tormented. I can't imagine how hard it was for you and you handled it all on your own. You figured out exactly who you were."

Finally I understand what he meant about looking up to me in high school. But still, it's hard to take in. I hated being teased but I felt like I couldn't control the things that made me a source of ridicule. Later as I became an adult I was able to erase any aspect of my personality that I thought was a weakness. But talking to Tack about his kid makes me wonder why the categories ever existed. "Jules will figure it out," I say. They seem more self-possessed at six than I was at sixteen. "It sounds to me like you're a pretty amazing father."

"Does it? When it takes the courage of your little kid to teach you to stop living a lie, I'm not sure I'm up for father of the year."

I look over at him and say, "Well, I think you are."

His pants are rolled up to his knees as ripples of water dance around his feet. He looks me dead in the eye and says, "Gurl, puhleeze." He waves his hand behind his shoulder in a pantomime hair flip and we both immediately laugh. I've never seen Tack do that before and it cracks me up. The mood changes from serious confessional to playful and winsome. The heavy secret that has kept us both chained to the ocean floor feels like it has dissolved suddenly. I feel giddy with celebration and paddle my feet in the water.

"Careful, you're gonna soak me," he says.

"Didn't Kevin say Shinrin-yoku means forest…" I take a dramatic pause "…bathing." I sweep my foot across the surface of the stream, covering him in a cool spray of spring water.

"Heeeey!" he yells and bends over to reach the water with his cupped hand. A wave of icy wetness covers me. The temperature has gone up at least a few degrees since we've been in the clearing and while the trees create a stunning canopy of leaves it's still getting sticky.

"That feels great," I say, bending over to scoop some water and pour a handful over my head.

Tack jumps up and stands over me. "Last one in has to scrub the soup pot after I make chili." He peels off his tank top to reveal his washboard abs covered in soft patches of blond hair. He puts his hand on the buckle of his jeans.

"What are you doing?" I ask, pulling my almost frozen toes out of the water.

"You said it feels great and Kevin said the water is deep enough here for skinny-dipping so you better start taking off those clothes or you'll have dishpan hands for a week." Tack opens his pants and his dick just flops out and swings under him. Of course he still doesn't wear underwear. That's so Tack. I try not to stare but who am I kidding? I can't take my eyes off the thing. "Let's go, Vince," he says.

I start taking off my clothes as quickly as I can, not because I'm worried about dish duty but because I don't want to take off my pants to reveal the boner that's pointing straight up to the sky like a sunflower searching for light. The water is so cold I know I won't have to worry once I am submerged.

Tack is still yanking on a pant leg when I say, "Oh, look—a newborn fawn down on the other side of the river." I point downstream and across the way. Tack, whose love for animals is borderline obsessive, stops and asks, "Where?"

I take that opportunity to strip off the rest of my clothes, look for the part of the stream that is the deepest and do a massive cannonball into the water.

Chapter Twenty

Tack

"You sneaky little shit," I yell at Vince as he treads water beneath me. I pull off the last few inches of my jeans and tell him to watch out. I take a few running steps off the ledge, pull my legs to my chest and jump in a few feet away from him. Under the water I quickly open my eyes and see that despite the cold water Vince still has a significant chubby. Good to know.

I push myself out of the water and the cold shock slowly becomes a refreshing chill. The sunlight filters through the leaves and it feels like our own private country oasis. I swim back over to the rock where Vince is moored and treading water. I make sure my strokes are long and high so he can see as much of my muscle as possible. I'm not beefy like he is but I know I'm in pretty good shape and I might as well show it off.

I grab the rock above me and we're face to face. Naked. I've gotten a lot off my chest today and it makes me feel light and open to anything. I kick my legs back and forth underneath me and the frigid cold of the deeper water swirls around my lower body while the humidity engulfs my head and all of the body parts above the water. The contrast almost makes me dizzy. I tread water just looking at Vince. He seems more naked today than he has since he showed up and not just because he isn't wearing any clothes. The macho bravado that kept him at a distance seems to have weakened a bit. His hair droops over his forehead and he isn't wearing a fitted dress shirt that has been perfectly tailored to stretch over every thick muscle in his arms.

Vince dips under the water and when he bobs up he pushes his hair back from his face and the water drips off his thick stubble. He bites his lip and I can tell he is fighting a gentle smile. He loses and the corners of his mouth push across his face. I smile back but I don't make any attempt to hide it. I let it shine across my face. I want him to know how happy I am to be here with him, for us to be together like this.

"Thank you, for letting me open up about myself."

"No problem," he says a bit more coldly than I would like. But I can't let this moment pass without letting him know how much it means to me.

I want to show him.

I plunge under the water and let the cold deliver a jolt

to my entire body. When I rise out of the water my mouth searches for his and I kiss him on the lips. At first he is tentative. I'm sure it's a surprise but also not really a surprise. I flash to my hand almost touching his in the truck, the way he looked at me on the side of the road, his eyes through the crack in the door during my first long shower in the suite. As my tongue gently moves against his lips I feel his mouth open. His tongue moves past mine and as soon as we are connected my whole body responds. He turns his head to the side and I turn mine in the opposite direction so we can go deeper. We both have an arm stretched above, holding the rock, and our feet are paddling to keep us afloat. Our mouths are connected. I take my free arm and go to hold him but he dissolves in front of me, dipping down below the surface.

It feels like I'm waking up from a dream but he appears again. The water drips down his face and off his nose and chin and he looks at me with confusion but I can tell there is a smile growing in his face. He might be fighting it but there is no denying it. Vince and I are locked together finally. I can't stop exploring his mouth with my own, going deeper inside him and unlocking places I never thought I would explore.

We tread water facing each other. The sunlight bounces and refracts as it hits the ripples in the stream. A rush of wind rustles the leaves and birds call out to each other in the distance. There is a world of life around us but in this moment all that is in front of me is Vince.

"I'm glad you decided to move back," I say. He smiles at me as the sunshine makes the water dripping off his face look like shiny diamonds. Right now he's just my old pal Vinny. Or maybe he's more than that.

"Tack, I need to tell you…" he starts but as soon as his lips start to move mine move closer to his and he stops speaking. He opens his mouth, gently inviting me to kiss him again. This time our tongues are more aggressive. The first kiss was tentative but this one has no hesitation in it at all. It's a drink of water after a drought, a gasp of air above the clouds. We are so close that if I move my hips enough I could swing my dick against him but I keep my hand on his waist and my groin a safe distance away so I can focus on his mouth.

I remember he was actually trying to tell me something so I summon my strength to pull my mouth away from his.

"What?" I ask.

"What what?" he asks back. I take it as a good sign that the kiss forced him to forget whatever he was going to tell me.

"Nothing," I say and kiss him again.

"Yoohoooo," I hear from just beyond the trees. "If anybody is naked, now would be the time to get decent," Kevin yells from a few yards away. "Or not—as you see fit."

Vince releases his hand from the rock and dives underwater. I feel his feet push water against my torso and he reappears a few yards away from me, close to the shore.

"We better get going," he says, wading out and walking back to where our clothes are sitting in lifeless piles baking in the sun. I can hear Kevin getting closer.

"Vince," I yell across the stream. "It's just Kevin. He's

seen more naked men than an army doctor. He doesn't care."

He scrambles to the rock and uses his tank top as a towel to dry off enough to put his underwear back on. I laugh to myself and smile. I knew he was in there somewhere, the shy boy on the rock, freaking out that someone might see him naked. Vince walks around preening and strutting. I don't mind it but it's all a show. Watching him vulnerable and real is such a turn-on, so much more than his bulging biceps and thick thighs.

"Damn, we missed the show," Kevin says as he makes his way to the clearing, Evan at his side. They both look at Vince who has managed to yank on both his underwear and his top. The material clings to him like a toga on a Greek statue so even though the show is over there isn't much imagination needed to see how stunning Vince's body is.

"Hey," I yell from the water. "I haven't made my exit yet. You might get lucky."

Kevin claps his hands and Evan gives him a look before approaching Vince. "Hello, I'm Evan. I apologize for my husband, who sometimes thinks he's running a burlesque show and not an organic farm." They shake hands. "Kevin tells me you might be interested in some of our produce and dairy. Let's head up to the office and see if we can work something out."

"Perfect," Vince says and they head up to the farmhouse.

Kevin remains standing on the rock, staring at me and waiting for his show.

"Kevin!" Evan yells from beyond the clearing. Kevin

rolls his eyes and walks away from the stream. "Tack, we'll meet you up there."

Alone in the stream, I let the cold water run over my body and push my dick against my thigh. I can feel the head bounce and I can't help thinking about Vince and how it felt to kiss him and mean it. It was the kiss of two men who know who they are, or at least two men who think they know who they are. Vince's body is enough for any jerk-off fantasy but I can't help thinking about his eyes as he was scurrying to get dressed. The laser focus was gone and replaced with an openness that made me want to dive in.

I lift myself out of the water and crawl onto the smooth surface of the biggest boulder I can find. The surface is hot but not scalding so I let it warm my back as the sun evaporates the water droplets on the front of my body. I can't stop thinking about the kiss. It was pretty bold of me but as soon as we started taking off our clothes I knew all bets were off. It wasn't just seeing Vince naked although that was clearly a turn-on, it was also talking with him like we did when were kids. What we talk about is totally different now but the connection is the same and when my hands move down to my crotch I see that my reaction is *exactly* the same.

I thought I would never see him again once he left town. Now he's back and making me have feelings I didn't know I would feel. Feelings that cracked open all those years ago but I fought so hard to shift. But here they are, rushing out of me like water that's been released from behind a dam. I've kissed enough guys since I came out to realize not many make you feel the way Vince makes me feel. No one has ever made me feel the way Vince makes me feel and I doubt anyone else ever could.

I scoop up some water in my hand and pour it over my face. The water tingles over the parts of my cheek that his scruff brushed against. Kissing him has not only stirred emotions in me that I haven't felt in years, it's strengthened my resolve to see this through. There is something there. I know it might not happen overnight and he's got this big tough guy act in lockdown but he can't keep it up forever, can he? I can't believe I've had to wait this long to have all these feelings again. I'm not about to let them slip through my fingers a second time.

The early afternoon sun starts to sting so I slide off the rock and back into the stream. The sudden rush of cold finally makes my dick behave. I float on my back and stare up at the canopy of glowing green leaves blocking the sun from my eyes. It feels great to be exactly where I'm supposed to be.

Chapter Twenty-One

"Yes. That's exactly where I want to be," I say without really thinking.

"Good," Barry says. "FunTyme wants to move on this project. You could be back in New York by Labor Day. Think you can make the number attractive? I know this is a tight deadline." I'm walking back to meet Tack at his truck after discussing orders with Kevin and Evan. I find a spot off the path from the office where I have enough of a signal to clarify what Barry's just said.

"End of August?" I ask.

"Right. They don't like to wait and they'll move to another property if your numbers aren't impressive by then. I'll email you over some of the details of the prospectus.

They're just starting to look at how to structure some of this so it should give you a benchmark."

"Great." I wanted to be out of here by the end of the summer anyway. This just means I'll have to work a little harder to make sure I meet that deadline.

"I know you'll do what it takes. I'm about to board and I got my eye on the flight attendant for my *laid* over in Frankfurt." He laughs like a fifth grader telling a fart joke and hangs up.

I turn off my phone completely and put it in my pocket. I have too many worlds colliding and I don't want another one to enter.

I walk back to the truck and try to focus on what I need to do to make the numbers look good to FunTyme but thoughts of Tack creep back in. I take my hand and run it along the smooth finish of his truck and lean against the hood. The dam between my heart and my head that I've spent most of my adult life building suddenly cracks and I can't stop it.

The kiss. I touch the middle of my lower lip and brush the exact spot where we connected. How many times have I fantasized about his kiss—sat in bed as a teenager and tried to wish it into being?

The feel of his mouth on mine.

The moment his hands searched through the water for my waist.

The way our noses gently bumped until our bodies were in sync.

But what does it mean? Was it the ending to something

that started a long time ago or was it an invitation to a beginning?

"You ready to go?"

I turn around to see Tack smiling at me. His hair has dried in such a way that it points in a dozen different directions. The sun is behind him so each point glows just enough to make it look like he's wearing a crown. But I can't help focusing on his lips. I finally kissed those lips today.

I get in the truck without saying a word and he hops in and puts the key in the ignition. Before he turns over the motor he stops and turns to me. "Do you want to talk about it?"

I look down at my lap and notice the folder of information Kevin and Evan gave me during our meeting.

"The order? No, not until I make sure I can make the numbers work. I'll review their wholesale catalog on the drive back."

"You think I want to talk about the order?" he asks. I know he wants to talk about the kiss but I can't.

"Of course, what else is there to talk about?" I look over at him, hoping I sound convincing but knowing he can tell I'm avoiding the conversation. He turns the key in the ignition, starts the truck and turns on the radio.

This time Tack avoids the back roads and goes right to the closest highway without so much as a crack in his calm neutral expression. I keep my nose buried in the papers like I'm a religious scholar studying scripture. I'm grateful we are on the highway because it means he has to keep his eyes focused on the road and I can catch a glimpse of him every now and then.

Maybe if I hadn't just heard from Barry I would have talked about the kiss with him, but the fact is Barry just offered me the very thing I've been wanting. But that was before Tack picked me up on the side of the road and moved in with me. I was about to tell Tack that I have no intention of staying in New Hope when we were in the stream but then he kissed me again and logic tumbled away in the rapids.

I steal a glimpse of his profile and then go right back down to my papers. The afternoon sun is beginning to show on his face. His usual creamy skin has just a layer of pink developing on his cheeks and the number of freckles over the bridge of his nose has doubled.

Is there any possibility of seeing this through with Tack? He could never leave the country and once I sell the inn what would I do for work? There aren't a lot of international real estate investment teams in between the candle shops and trinket stores in New Hope.

"Do you mind if we make a quick stop?" Tack asks.

"No, not at all."

"We're going by the Kandy Kitchen and Jules loves their Scotchmallows."

The word *Scotchmallow* is like a pistol that fires off a memory.

"You mean the candies that are marshmallow covered in caramel that taste like sweet clouds and are wrapped in wax paper and when you buy four you get one free?"

The words shoot out of my mouth.

"I see you have not forgotten them. Would you like me to get you one?" he asks.

I want to ask him to buy out the entire stock but instead I say, "No. That's okay. I'll pass. Thank you." I'm trying to establish my boundaries.

He pulls over in front of the square brick building with white benches on each side of the door and the pink and white striped awning that goes across the entire building that hasn't changed since I was a kid. I keep studying the wholesale catalog until I see out of the corner of my eye that Tack is in the shop.

I watch him through the window looking over the sweets and pointing to different confections. Tack is a good dad. It sounds like he really understands Jules for who they are and he's thoughtful stopping off to get them a treat. It makes me melt inside knowing Tack is so kind with his kid. I know Tack's dad never really showed him any affection.

I've never been involved with a guy who has kid. On the surface it seems like it would be a total hassle but listening to Tack talk about his child didn't make it sound like a hassle at all. I liked hearing about Jules and the challenges of raising a kid and how Tack meets those challenges. It wasn't a turnoff. If anything, it made me more attracted to him.

"Stop it," I say out loud. It doesn't matter. I'm not getting involved with Tack. I'm selling the inn and going back to New York by the end of the summer. Not to mention, I would be a disaster as a stepdad. I'd demand quiet when I'm studying an annual report and lose my temper when I didn't get it. I wouldn't know how to talk to a kid at all. I'm barely able to have normal conversations outside of a business setting. I'd be snarky and flip or overly condescending. Still, Jules sounds like an incredible kid and I wonder if I might be able to rise to the occasion.

Tack comes out of the shop and I take my little fantasy and shove it as deep down as I can so it doesn't percolate to the top of my mind again. He gets in the truck and puts two paper bags on his lap. "These are for Jules," he says, placing one in the back. "These are for you," he says, smiling at me and handing me the bag.

I look inside. A Scotchmallow and all its caramelly goodness sits wrapped in wax paper at the bottom of the bag.

"See," Tack says, starting his truck and pulling out of the parking lot. "I'm not such a bad guy."

No, Tack. Maybe you aren't at all. Behind him the afternoon sun creates a halo that makes his sweet face look even more angelic. Even the solar system is on this guy's side.

I look inside the bag again and notice a bright pink piece of paper. I pull it out and ask, "What's this?"

"Oh, it's a flyer for the Annual Fudge Fest. They've been doing it for years. I thought your sweet tooth might enjoy it." He starts the truck and pulls out of the parking lot.

The flyer has puffy lettering and so many exclamation points it can be heard on the other side of the river. It announces: "Twelfth Annual Kandy Kitchen Fudge Festival. Come one, come all. Labor Day Weekend."

Labor Day. I'm planning to be out of here by then. I quickly put the flyer back in the bag next to the candy. Suddenly I've lost my appetite.

Chapter Twenty-Two

Tack

"What are you doing?" I open the door to my bedroom and through my barely awake squinting eyes spot Vince on his knees hammering on the bathroom door. We've stayed up way beyond midnight every night for the past week working together to get ready for the re-reopening. Each night I want to follow him to his bedroom when we're done but despite my best game he remains unwilling to talk about what's happening between us.

He turns to look at me and then quickly turns back to the door like he has seen something he shouldn't. I'm only wearing a pair of boxers but after our skinny-dipping session I barely think we can return to modesty.

"I'm fixing the door," he says and keeps banging. "It won't close because the hinge has been painted over so I took it out, stripped it and now I'm putting it back."

"Really? Hammering. That was the item on your list you thought best for the morning. Maybe that could be an afternoon event."

"We don't have much privacy around here and I thought you might appreciate a door that closes."

Quite the opposite. There's a spot at the table by the window where I can get a nice view of Vince as he moves from shaving at the sink to hopping in the shower. I've been using that image to get through our daily meetings where I flirt as hard as possible but try not to cross the line. I feel like I'm testing the brakes of a race car.

Vince is squatting on the floor and his ass sticks out like a balloon on a carnival dartboard. There's no way anyone would call this guy Skinny Vinny now. I get he's worked hard to have the quintessential masculine physique but it also makes me sad. Does he think people like him for what he has attained? His gym body? His considerable bank account? I wonder if anyone in New York really sees him the way I do. I wonder if Vince will ever let me really see him. He can't keep up this macho bullshit show forever. Can't he see how it's keeping me out when all I want to do is get in?

I kneel down next to him. "Let me help you. You hold your hinge in place and I'll just hammer away," I say, staring at his ass the entire time I'm talking.

"Thanks. I've got this and you're right. I should do this later." He stands up, leaving me on the floor. I extend my hand signaling that I want a hand getting up. I don't need it but it's fun to torture Vince this way. I can see how hard he is resisting me and I can also see how bad a job he's doing. Vince extends his arm but quickly looks to the side to avoid eye contact. It doesn't matter. As soon as I grab his hand, I feel it and I know he must too.

After all those years our physical connection has finally been activated and there is no way to stop it. We both know it. The only difference is I'm not trying to resist it. I'm sure this impromptu fix-it job is one more attempt to keep us apart but it's going to take more than a bathroom door to stop me.

I squeeze his hand on the way up from the floor but once I'm standing he releases his grip and I don't let go. He turns to look at me and I smile at him, letting him know this is okay. We don't have to fight this any longer. He doesn't immediately pull his hand away and I take that as progress. Last week he would have snapped away on impulse. I raise my eyebrows just a bit to let him know resistance is futile.

"Did you get to finish that appetizer recipe you were working on? The one with the goat cheese?" he asks, switching gears purposefully.

"I did," I say.

"Great. Why don't you get dressed and we can go downstairs to do a tasting?"

"No need."

"You can't go downstairs dressed like that. It's…it's…" he stammers, looking my body up and down. I don't preen but I also don't make any attempt to cover myself up.

"It's what?" I ask, looking down at my naked chest,

wondering if he can see the growing erection in my boxer shorts.

"It's unhygienic. What if the health inspector did a spot inspection and they see my chef dressed like he's auditioning for a male strip club revue?"

I casually stretch my arms over my head in a way that I know accentuates the taut features of my midsection. "You mean Toby Horowitz? That health inspector? We played baseball for years together. This ain't nothing he hasn't seen before. He's on his third wife. He won't care. Unless the sight of my body makes it difficult for you to focus?" I ask, my voice full of playful mischief.

Vince's eyes linger on the patch of hair in the center of my chest for just a few seconds longer than I imagine he wants them to linger. Then he snaps out of it and shakes his head. "Wait a minute, Toby Horowitz became the health inspector for Bucks County?"

"Yeah, I know. Kind of a shock, right?"

"You mean the Toby Horowitz who I personally saw pick his nose and eat boogers multiple times during biology."

"Same guy," I say and nod my head. "But it proves my point." I grab a T-shirt that's hanging from a hook behind my bedroom door and pick up the first pair of basketball shorts I see on the floor.

"What point is that?" Vince asks.

"People can change and some people can even stop picking their nose."

Vince lets out a laugh. I'm making progress so as a gesture of goodwill I throw on the shirt and we head downstairs.

★ ★ ★

"What do you think of this?" I ask, holding a forkful of my latest creation just in front of Vince's mouth. "It's roasted garlic and turnips from Iron Bridge Farm and goat cheese from Kevin's goats with black sesame seeds."

He opens his mouth and I slowly put the white sticky mess directly onto his tongue. We both pretend there is absolutely nothing sexual about what I'm doing.

"It's delicious. That. Whatever that is. That goes on the menu but keep it away from me or I won't stop eating." He throws his head back in surrender. "Ugh. Why is that goat cheese so fucking good? Last night I woke up at 3 a.m. and came down for a spoonful."

I give him a smirk. "A spoonful? Half the container was missing this morning."

"Was it?" he asks innocently.

There is a gentle silence between us. Vince's eyes are searching mine and I dive right into his. Maybe this is the moment to leap right over his walls and go deeper into those piercing inky eyes that I want to lose myself in. I'm about to test the sturdiness of his resistance when the creaky kitchen door interrupts my offense and Anita rolls in. She rolls right past me and up to Vince.

"Where the hell are the pride flags? What did you do?"

"You took down the pride flags?" I ask.

"They were worn and faded," Vince explains.

Anita gives Vince a look like she doesn't completely believe him. "I just came back from the printer's with the new menus and I had them print up a one page version for the both of you."

"I don't need a cheat sheet. I think I can remember everything on the menu," I say with an unfiltered sarcasm.

"Am I the only one who can keep things going around here? Leave it to the Indian woman in the wheelchair to keep the ship from sinking," she says and rolls over to the desk where she keeps invoices and receipts.

"Tomorrow is the Tinicum Fourth of July Festival," she says, waving an overstuffed folder at us. "You two have already agreed to hand out our new menu for the grand reopening next week."

"Oh, right," I say, realizing this is the perfect opportunity to unleash my secret weapon. Vince might be able to resist my charm but I also happen to be the dad of the most amazing kid in the world. "The festival is Jules's favorite thing each summer. There's a petting zoo that they love and last year they made some kind of wand with sparkles and streamers at the kids' craft table. It's my day with Jules already so this is perfect."

"Great, looks like you are already going so it won't be a problem. I've got some errands to run, so I'm sure you don't need me," Vince says, making it clear that he does not want to be involved.

"Do you see how many menus I have printed? In color. I got a deal but they still cost a fortune. You are both going," Anita says, handing the folder off to Vince.

"Fortune, did you say?" he asks. I've been trying to appeal to his bottom but Anita is making more headway with his bottom line.

"Fortune," she says. "The festival is one of the biggest in Bucks County and the timing couldn't be better. In case you forgot, we have the restaurant reboot or re-reopening or whatever you want to call it coming up."

"You're with your kid tomorrow. It's a holiday. I don't want to intrude."

"Are you kidding? I've told Jules all about you. They would love to meet you. It will be fun and I'd love to have you meet them." *You are falling right into my plan, Vince, and you may not even know it.*

"Um…" He hesitates but he doesn't really have a choice.

"It's settled," Anita says like a judge slamming her gavel as she renders a verdict. "Don't come home until that folder is empty."

I take the folder from Anita and look at Vince. Idyllic country fair. Me and my adorable kid on the offense. Vince's defense doesn't stand a chance.

Chapter Twenty-Three

Jules has Tack's eyes—sky blue circles with gray sparks around the center. I was nervous about meeting them for a million different reasons but the second I get in Tack's truck Jules starts asking me questions, singing me songs from school and telling me made-up stories. They are clearly amped up for the Fourth of July festival and their energy is very infectious. They have this joy about them and it makes me feel playful—something I haven't felt in a very long time.

"Our principal had a pet hippo," I say as we drive up River Road in Tack's truck with Jules sitting between us. I roll down the window and a steady rush of morning summer air rushes through the cab. A steep rock formation is on our left and on the right, I can see some early morning kayakers making their way down the river. Jules hangs on Tack. Tack is beaming. He's also driving more carefully than I have ever seen him before. I haven't hit my head on the roof once.

"Pet hippo?" Jules asks.

"Yep," I say. "Kept him half the time in the swimming pool and the other half on the soccer field."

"Oh, is that how you and my dad know each other? Did you play sports? My dad played football. And track."

"Yeah, I know," I say. "But I didn't really play any sports. I don't like them."

"Me neither," Jules says as they move their grip from Tack's arm to my hand.

The suddenness of this makes me uncomfortable but I'm not so much of an asshole as to push away a child's affection. Is this okay with Tack? I look over at him and he is smiling so brightly he could light the way if a full eclipse were in the forecast.

This morning I was nervous about meeting Jules because I'm not really good with kids. I haven't really been around that many and I generally keep my distance. I guess I don't have very good memories of being a kid myself so it's hard for me not to be tense around children. I'm always thinking they're going to see me as a fraud, see past my exterior to something inside that is broken. But Jules has this honesty about them that isn't scary, it's affirming. I can understand how Jules's energy made Tack serious about coming out.

Jules continues telling a story to us about their new camp and how they let them take whatever craft they want instead of making them play the sports. They talk about loving things with feathers that sparkle, applesauce when it has cinnamon in it and that they want to drive the world's biggest dump truck when they are older.

"I thought you wanted to drive old Axel here?" Tack asks Jules with a pretend frown on his face.

"Sure, Dad. Maybe after the dump truck," Jules says and then they whisper in my ear, "Don't say anything bad about the truck. Dad is totally in love with Axel. You just have to go with it."

"I got it," I whisper back and nod my head. Tack rubs the top of Jules's head and then smiles at me and in that moment my biggest fear is realized before we are even out of the truck. Sure, I was nervous about being around a kid but what really terrified me was how I would feel seeing Tack with Jules. I've been working so hard to keep an emotional wall between us and not let that intimacy from the stream return but here it is rushing in like the wind from the open window.

"I knew you'd understand," Jules says and Tack lets out a low chuckle. There is already a cozy dynamic with all three of us and I roll up the window as quickly as possible to stop the breeze but I think it might be too late.

The Fourth of July festival is buzzing by the time we get there. Red, white and blue bunting decorates the weathered wood barn in the center of the park. The massive barn doors are open, revealing the cavernous space that has been turned into a temporary art gallery. There are stalls with local artists, community organizations and activities for kids and families scattered around. A midsummer breeze makes the American flags that dot the fairground wave gently. Some food trucks are gathered by the entrance near the picnic tables covered with red and white tablecloths, and the hot dogs and fry oil already make the air smell delicious but fattening.

"Let's go visit Paul," Jules says, grabbing my hand.

"It looks like you've made a friend," Tack says as Jules runs ahead of me, pulling my arm.

"No," they say. "I want you both to come." Jules continues holding my hand with their right arm and then grabs their dad's hand with their left so they are in the middle between us. The three of us run together and without saying a word we both swing Jules's arms so they rise up a few inches in the air. They cackle with laughter. We get to the petting zoo and Jules decides to make sure each animal gets a fair share of food and the same amount of petting.

"Do you want to go in the bouncy castle?" Tack asks.

"No," Jules says with a serious look on their face. They look over at the other kids jumping and laughing. I immediately notice that kids have to be with an adult in the petting zoo but the bouncy attractions are kids only. I notice the look of concern on their face. I can tell Jules is unsure about being with the other kids without their dad around.

"But this morning you said that was what you wanted to do most after feeding Paul."

"I know," they say. I can sense the nervousness in their voice.

"I have an idea," I say. "Why don't we see who can make the most magical wand in the crafts tent? I bet your dad doesn't know a rhinestone from a rock."

"Yeah!" Jules shouts and within a few minutes all six of our hands are covered in glitter, glue and rhinestones.

By the middle of the afternoon the festival is swarming with people. We've handed out plenty of menus for The Hideaway and Tack does a great job of selling and describing his creations. We've visited the petting zoo a number of times, eaten corn dogs, cotton candy and lemonade, looked at the photos and paintings at the art exhibit in the barn, and Jules made a sword with a jeweled handle and feathers on the tip so it "doesn't hurt anybody" after we each finished our wands.

Walking around the festival I think about when I was growing up how I hated everything about this area. I thought it was so boring and Podunk. I thought I would never find a way to be a part of it. I was sure there would be better things waiting for me in a big city like New York but after a day here with Tack and Jules now I wonder if those things are just different, not better.

"I think maybe I want to go in the bouncy castle now. Can I?" Jules asks Tack.

"Are you sure?" Tack asks, seeing that it's even more crowded with kids. "Do you want us to go over there with you?"

"No, you guys can wait here." Tack gives them the okay and they run over, kick off their shoes and start bouncing before they even get inside. Tack and I sit next to each other in a quiet spot across from the bouncy castle.

"I'm exhausted," I say and lean back on the bench and spread myself for a quick stretch that I'm too tired to finish.

"Cooking for a full dining room is nothing compared to keeping up with Jules."

I can hear music coming from a small brass band playing at a bandshell on the other side of the festival. It's some kind of patriotic march like you would hear at a parade. A gentle breeze sweeps across us and we both sigh almost in unison. We sit in our silence for a while. I've been waiting for a moment like this to return, one where we are connected without talking. It's so easy to be around Tack. I can just relax for a few moments. I never thought there was a place for me in picture-perfect Americana but maybe that frame has shifted recently and become more inclusive. Maybe I can belong in places where I never thought I was allowed.

A clown making balloon animals pops a poodle's head right in front of us and it breaks the spell.

"You ever think about having one?" Tack asks.

"A balloon animal?"

"No," he says, slapping me playfully on the arm. "A kid. Have you ever thought about having a kid?"

No one has ever asked me that before. I've always been too focused on success to really give it serious thought.

"I mean, I know you don't want a boyfriend or a husband. Your career comes first and all, but I just thought it might have crossed your mind at some point."

I still don't know how to answer him. I never really thought it was something realistic to consider. I know gay men adopt and have surrogates but generally you need a partner for that and I never thought that was part of my plan.

"If I did have a kid, I know I would want them to have a different life than I did."

"In what way?"

All a kid like Jules really needs is someone to listen to them. I know that's what I needed. I wouldn't need to give Jules advice about what to do or how to act. I'd just wait until they came home from school and listen to everything they had to say. I look at Tack and say, "I'd ask questions about how they feel and their friends and what they like to do and what scares them. I'd make sure they felt heard in every way. I would raise a kid to be themselves. To not be scared of anything. I'd protect them from all the people in the world who would want them to fit in." I speak firmly and decisively. Tack is listening to me with his ears but keeping one eye on his kid in the bounce house. "Like you're doing with Jules," I say.

"Thanks, Vince. That means a lot to me. It definitely sounds like we are on the same page about what a kid needs."

I never thought Tack could be any sexier. I've fantasized about his body since I was a teenager and that fantasy has never gotten old. But there is something about seeing how tender he is with Jules and knowing that he is finally out to the world that makes me want him more deeply than I have ever imagined. The thought of us being on the same page about raising a kid makes my head spin.

A breeze sweeps across our faces and I let it blow my hair across my forehead without any resistance. It's about two months until Labor Day and I can't keep this fight up that long. "About the other day," I start but it takes a second to get up my courage. "In the stream."

"I know you don't want to talk about it. I get it," he

says and I see his bottom lip rise as a frown appears across his face.

"No, it's not. I mean… I'm sorry I got so weird after and shut you out. That's not what I want to do."

"What do you want, Vince?" he says, looking at me.

His hand is resting on the bench just a few inches from mine. Inch by inch I move closer to his until his pinky is aligned with mine. As soon as our skin connects he smiles. He keeps looking ahead but I know the connection is powerful. It's not like kissing in the stream. That was pure sexual heat. This is different.

I take my hand and move it on top of his. It lands there for just a second before he turns his over so that my hand is in his palm and then he covers it with his fingers. We are sitting on a bench at the Tinicum Fourth of July Festival and now we are both smiling.

Chapter Twenty-Four

Tack

"Wait. Where are you going?" Vince asks as I drive past The Hideaway after dropping off Jules with Evie. The sun has finally left the midsummer sky but there is still a pink and golden hue hanging on to the last moments of the holiday.

"I'm not ready for today to end. How about you?" I ask.

Vince moves his hand to the top of my thigh and I move my right hand down from the steering wheel to meet his. "No, I'm not ready either, but where are we going?" he asks.

"I know a spot I've been wanting to take you to for a very, very long time." The farther we get from town the louder the sounds of crickets and other woodland creatures become. I softly brush the top of his hands with my fingers as rows of pristine Victorian homes transition to trees and countryside. The pastel tones of evening become the inky darkness of night. It feels like we are the only two people in the world.

I pull over to the old little league field by the river that hasn't been used since I was in middle school. Patches of grass have grown over the sandy infield and I drive right down the middle of it to the center of the park.

"You get the best view of them here and it's about to hit peak season." I reach behind Vince and grab a wool plaid blanket. "Come on," I say softly and lead him to the bed of the pickup truck where I unfold the blanket, making a soft nest for us. We sit next to each other and watch as the show begins.

It takes a second for our eyes to adjust and then they appear. Little blinks of orange light appear and disappear in random order. Something about this field being near the river and next to a forest reserve makes this spot a paradise for lightning bugs. We lie down on the blanket next to each other and stare up holding hands. The sky seems to be filled with them now. Electric orange sequins dot the darkness. It's serenely beautiful and awe-inspiring. The tails glow and dim so gently and the pattern they make across the sky is like electric confetti that has been suspended in time. We hear fireworks far off in the distance but we have our own private show.

Vince squeezes my hand as the fireflies create a force field around us.

"Thank you for bringing me here. I never knew a baseball diamond could become so magical." Orange glows appear, disappear and reappear. I roll on my side and Vince does the same. I want to kiss him so badly. I want us to take this further but I need to be patient. I need to let him make the next move. There is just enough moonlight to stare into his dark brown eyes that sometimes look like rich leather but tonight look like melting chocolate. Just as I'm beginning to think I could stay looking at him this way forever he makes his move. He reaches for my mouth with his. It's an easy kiss. Slow and comfortable like a favorite T-shirt you've found in the back of your closet. This doesn't feel like it's about the past. This feels like a new beginning, at least to me.

I press my body against his. I want to feel every inch of it on mine. I want to be closer to him than I have ever been before. My hands move across his chest, feeling his big muscles and moving my fingers through his thick hair. I know he uses his body to buffer himself from the world but in this moment it feels like he is giving me permission to go beyond that, to see him and feel him for who he is.

We stay with our mouths connected. At first, his tongue is tentative and unsure of the landscape, then it goes deeper in mine, exploring parts of me that have been dormant like a crop of broad beans waiting for the frost to end. My tongue explores his mouth also but mine lacks any hesitation whatsoever. I may not have been down this route yet but it feels like I've always known his road map.

Vince reaches for my pants and I don't wait for him to take them off. I pull them down to my ankles and get at least one foot out so I can be more mobile. Before I can get my pants off Vince is diving for my dick. He puts it in his mouth and I think I might shoot immediately. I move my hands through his hair and whisper, "Slow down."

"I can't," he says. "I've waited most of my life for this."

I put my hand on his chin and gently tilt his head up so we're looking at each other. "So have I, Vince. So have I."

He rips the other leg of my pants off over my foot. He spreads my legs with his arms and dives for my dick again. I focus on the pleasure and that helps me fight an immediate orgasm. He takes all of my dick into his mouth and the sensation is wet and hot and so intense that I forget about the damn butterflies or fireflies or whatever they are illuminating this incredible blow job.

But I don't want Vince to have all the fun. I unbuckle his belt and help him slide off his pants. I shift myself so he still has access to my dick but I am also in front of his dick. He's already been pulling on it so it's full and hard. His is shorter than mine but much thicker, so thick I hesitate, thinking I might not be able to get my mouth around it. My jaw stretches open. Challenge accepted. I'm all over his dick with my lips and tongue and my hands. All of my energy at that moment is on getting Vince to come. It's all I can think about until he levels up on my dick.

Vince starts putting his hand right next to his mouth as we sixty-nine, stroking deeper and sucking harder. The intense feeling happening down below is almost more than I can take but I don't let it distract me. I push my head up and down on his dick, letting it stretch open my jaw until

I think it will snap but I don't give a fuck. I just want to please him, to taste him, to be connected to…

"Oh man. Tack, Tack. I'm gonna… I'm so close…"

"Vince, babe, me too, I'm going…"

Vince comes across my lips and as soon as the first drop hits me my dick knows and covers him in my load.

He moans so loud I swear a few fireflies get frightened and fly away.

I laugh and it makes my stomach bounce by Vince's head and that seems to make him laugh too. We are on our backs lying head to toe and I feel his hand move down my thigh and reach for mine. I move my hand up and reach for his. It only takes a second for my breathing to slow down and I hear his breath slowing too until we are both breathing calmly. We begin inhaling and exhaling in sync. It feels good to be in sync. Finally.

Chapter Twenty-Five

Tack stands behind me and puts his arms around my waist and it makes my whole body vibrate. His hands slide over mine as I steady the mixing bowl on the counter with one hand and use the other to keep stirring with the whisk. I'm trying to help out in the kitchen before we officially open the doors for our re-reopening. I know I'm more of a nuisance than actual assistance but I can't stay away from Tack lately. I need to be near him.

"If you stir in a circle it doesn't let the oil emulsify with the vinegar. Try moving back and forth," he says and then grabs my whisking hand. Together we beat the ingredients until the puddles of mustard, balsamic and truffle oil combine to make Tack's signature vinaigrette. He takes a tasting spoon and dips it in the freshly made dressing and then brings it to my mouth.

"No, no," I say playfully, turning to face him. "I cooked, so you taste." He surrenders the tasting spoon from his hand to mine. "Open up."

He closes his eyes and I gently slide the spoon in his mouth. His lips wrap around it and a smile appears. "Delicious. My compliments to the chef."

"You *are* the chef," I say, unable to take my eyes off his lips.

"Oh, right," he says with an overexaggerated tone and I kiss him on the nose.

The door to the dining room pushes open and Anita rolls into the kitchen. "I think I liked it better when you two were playing at the emotional cage match thing. Will you give it a rest for five minutes? We are about to open."

Tack takes his hands off my waist and I feel the disconnect like a candle that has been temporarily snuffed. "We've got everything under control. There's nothing to worry about. It's going to be great." His voice doesn't convey an ounce of stress.

We've been working together to make sure tonight is the opposite of what happened on Steak Night. Everything has changed. Instead of advertising New York steaks we have focused on farm to table food. Tack has helped me to make relationships with many of the area suppliers. More importantly, though, we have made a relationship with each other. I have to admit we're working together well, and I'm enjoying it more than I'm completely ready to admit.

"How's the crowd?" I ask Anita. I know we are prepared but success depends on more than just preparation. We need customers.

"Around the block," Anita says proudly. I was nervous she wouldn't be able to drum up business after we disappointed so many people in June. Building trust is an important part of any business and regaining trust is always an uphill battle. But with persistence, I've learned lately, it is possible.

"I'll go help Anita at the door. We are officially open for business. Again," I say and follow Anita out to the dining room.

"Wait, wait," Tack says and walks over to me. "You can't officially open without this." He kisses me softly on the forehead.

I kiss him on the cheek and say, "You've got this." Then head out to the dining room to greet our first customers.

"How did we do?" Tack asks after finishing in the kitchen and taking off his apron. The controlled chaos of under an hour ago has transformed to a peaceful respite. He walks over to where I'm sitting going over the receipts for the night and puts his hands on the space between my neck and shoulders and starts massaging my tired muscles. I take my hand off my calculator and raise it up to my shoulder to meet his. He holds it softly.

"These receipts don't lie. It was an amazing night. Everyone was raving about the food. The vibe in the dining room was great."

"Vince, I'm so impressed with what you've done." Tack seeing me as successful means a lot to me. I take a half second to bask in it. "This place was struggling for a long time. Everyone was worried about it being bought up by some chain."

"Oh, really?" I ask, trying to convey surprise in my voice. I should take this opportunity to tell Tack the truth. The fact is I was—am, definitely am—planning to sell the place. At least I'm pretty sure I am. I think I am or I might. I push the very thought of business and investments out of my mind because I don't want to stop feeling the connection between us. I know I need to tell him before they make an offer or before the contracts come in but there is still time. It's not like I told him I plan to hold on to The Hideaway forever. He knows I have a life back in New York but at this moment that all feels very far away. I know I need to get back to it but right now I'm not in a hurry. I just want to sit back and hear Tack go on about what a success I am.

"Yeah, but seeing that dining room full was amazing. Look at the number of dinners we sold tonight. You have done the impossible. You're on your way to making The Hideaway Inn a success."

"No," I correct him. "*I'm* not." I tilt my head back to look up at him standing behind me. "We are," I say and pucker my lips. He reads the signal perfectly and lowers his lips to meet mine. "I loved watching you in the kitchen tonight. The orders came rolling in fast and you handled it all perfectly. No panic, just calm control. It's very sexy."

"How about you? I peeked into the dining room and saw you talking to the customers, making sure everyone was relaxing and enjoying themselves. I love seeing you as part of the community. It's very sexy." He moves to the chair next to me and plants another kiss on my lips. He lingers on my mouth and I hold his face in my hands.

"Wait," I say, switching back to business mode and pulling away quickly.

"What? What's wrong?" he asks.

"Nothing's wrong," I say and grab a pen from the table to make a note. "I want to make sure I remember to send flowers or do something nice for Evan and Kevin."

"It was very nice of them."

"It's one thing to show up for the opening but to leave in the middle of their meal to go back to the farm to restock our supply of goat cheese was beyond nice. Who knew we would have such a run on your goat cheese appetizer?"

"Those things were flying out of the kitchen. We couldn't have handled the second rush without them running back to the farm for a special delivery. We should have them over for dinner upstairs once everything is up and running. Maybe before or after their big party."

"What big party?"

"Evan and Kevin always throw this big Halloween party the weekend of the High Heels Race. Jules loves it. They told me this year they want to go as a s'more."

"Really? I bet they will make a fantastic s'more." Jules is an amazing kid. I've really enjoyed getting to know them. Tack gets to see them a lot, and since the Fourth of July festival I've been included in many of their summer outings. Jules has a wildly creative mind but they're also so unafraid of the world. I wish I was that way as a kid. I wish I was more that way now.

Then it hits me. Halloween is, of course, two months
after Labor Day. That had been my deadline for getting out
of here and back to New York. If the opening is any indication of projected income, The Hideaway could get a
very substantial offer from FunTyme.

On the other hand, maybe I don't have to flip the inn.
Maybe the profits would be enough to give me a decent
living here.

"You don't understand," Tack says, unaware of the mach-
inations I'm hosting in my head. "They want *us* to be a
s'more. Jules has claimed the marshmallow, of course, but
they want us to join them. Do you want to be the chocolate
bar or the graham cracker?" He rubs my dark scruff with
the back of his hand. "I think you're more of a chocolate,
but whatever you're feeling."

"Oh, us," I say and a smile instantly appears on my face.
Us. This is a different kind of us entirely. I've surrendered
to the fact that Tack and I are, at the moment, an *us* but
I hadn't considered the us that includes Jules. I thought I
would immediately bristle at the thought of being part of
a family unit in that way. It's never something I thought I
wanted. But quite the opposite feeling takes hold. I feel a
sense of harmony that comes from a place I didn't know
existed. Spending time with Jules has made me feel connected to both of them in a profound way, so being part
of their *us* feels really good. I'm touched that Jules would
want to include me and honored that Tack would invite me.

I look at Tack and see his eyes smiling back at me and
think about how I would look dressed up as a chocolate bar.

Chapter Twenty-Six

Tack's clothes, books for school, toiletries and various charging cables are still in his room across from the living area. Tack, however, is in my room, specifically, my bed. At first we pretended that the air-conditioning unit was stronger in my room so it was just more comfortable for him to sleep with me. I was concerned about how it might look for the owner to have the chef sleeping in his room, not that anyone would know. After the way I left the corporate world, I'm more conscious of the power dynamics in the bedroom.

But the dynamic between us isn't boss and employee at all. It feels like we are partners in every sense of the word. We handle completely different tasks downstairs yet we need each other to make the whole operation run. It's the same upstairs. I always thought Tack was his best outdoors but it turns out he excels in both the kitchen and the bedroom. We couldn't have the restaurant doing as well as it's doing without his talent and we couldn't have my libido as satisfied as it is without it as well.

Tack is still in bed when I get up and unfortunately a sheet is covering up some of his best parts. I consider jumping into bed and picking up where we left off last night but the dining room was packed from open to close and I know he almost passed out after receiving one of the best blow jobs I've ever given. Giving him the opportunity to release after such a busy night felt like more than just getting off. It felt like connecting and that made it even hotter.

I grab the package I need for my errand and close the door gently so Tack can rest. As soon as I am out of the inn I see Steve, the contractor working on the rooms.

"Vince, we have to talk," he says.

"Uh-oh. Did you need to replace those pipes?" I ask. He showed me a section of plumbing a few weeks ago that looked like it had been installed before plumbing had been invented.

"No, actually. That worked out. The place is solid. It's one of my guys." Steve wipes some sweat off his forehead with a bandana. "His kid has to have a surgery. Nothing major but it is urgent and he needs to be off the job for a week or two. Maybe more. I could replace him to finish on time but I know he needs the money for the bills and he's my best guy. I said I would talk to you because it would mean a delay. I know I promised you Labor Day."

A year ago if a contractor came to me and said there was

a delay because of the personal life of one of his employees. I'd have fired the whole crew and found one that could do the work without issues. But I can't even imagine doing that here and now.

"Is it Manny?" I ask since I've seen his kid with him at work a few times.

"Yes, his son. He's been on the job site."

"Tell him I'm very sorry. Let's see what we can figure out."

The bells above the door at the bookstore ring as I enter. Toula is behind the register reading. Her hair is different than it was when I saw her at the start of the summer. She has a bigger curl and longer bangs. She turns the page of her book and I can hear the orchestra of wooden bracelets she is wearing make a hollow cascade of notes.

"Well, now that you are making a success of it I was hoping I would see you more. I just turned the kettle on. I'll bring you a cup," Toula says, coming out from around the register. It's the middle of August and should reach near a hundred today but Toula would never take a visitor without tea. I go to sit in my chair. "Anita tells me there have been some good reviews on social media and that Tack is creating some delicious masterpieces in the kitchen."

"He is. You should stop by. His food is really incredible," I say. She grabs a tray with the tea service and sits across from me. I look out the window and New Hope is just beginning to stir. It's a weekday so it's mostly locals taking care of errands and some day-trippers playing hooky from work. I see Arthur, the owner of The Beautiful Things

Shoppe, unrolling the awning in anticipation of a sunny day. Toula waves to him and he waves back.

"He's turning over the shop to Danny." Toula sighs. She pours me a cup of tea and I can smell the bouquet of chamomile immediately.

"Who?"

"Oh, this very nice young man who collects all sorts of unusual things like toys from something called a Happy Meal. Do you know what that is? It sounds divine. A *happy* meal?"

"Yes," I chuckle. "Everyone knows what that is." Toula's world is books, ideas and love. She doesn't really have a relationship with fast food promotions. "I got you something," I say and show her the small brown package I have tied up with string.

"I knew you were still that sweet boy." She smiles at me gently as I take a sip of tea. I don't feel the need to repel any mention of sweetness. I realize she is trying to pay me a compliment and I just take it in and ask her to open her gift.

She uses one of her aqua painted nails to break the string and then quickly tears open the brown paper. Presents are not usually my thing. I'm not great at remembering to give them and I hate receiving them. I never know how to react and I'm always scared the giver is going to see through any fake reaction. Toula squeals with a giggle and I know her reaction isn't fake.

"Oh, dear boy, you have no idea how much I need these poems right now." She runs her fingers over the cover and slowly touches each word in the title, *The Open Skies* by Barbara Guest. I know Toula loves Guest. She's one of my favorites as well. First editions of her books are rare so when I saw this at the used book tent at the Fourth of July festival, I grabbed it.

"I wanted to apologize for the last time we saw each other," I say sheepishly. I walked out in anger and Toula didn't deserve that. I'm truly embarrassed by my behavior. She was trying to help me like she always has and I was too stubborn to see it.

"Pish-posh," she says, waving her hand away. "You were acclimating. It's part of the journey." She dives back to the book. Toula knows exactly how to forgive someone. She accepts people for who they are so she doesn't have to draw it out or get defensive.

"You know," Toula begins as if she is about to tell me a secret, "Barbara Guest said the most wonderful thing about how poems are created."

I know exactly what she said. Toula has told me at least a hundred times but I want to let her tell me again. "What?" I ask.

"She says that the poem finds itself through the writing of the poem." Toula almost giggles she loves this idea so much. "Our lives are about living through them. We too must find ourselves."

I nod and let the thought enter my mind. A customer from the back brings a short stack of books to the register. Toula gets up from her rocker but it doesn't stop her from continuing our conversation. "Now tell me about you and Tack," she says as she rings up the sale and hands the customer back her credit card. I cringe thinking about this stranger knowing anything about my personal life. I wait for the woman to say thank you and leave before responding.

"There is no me and Tack," I say. At best this is a summer fling. I still haven't told anyone that I plan to have the inn listed for sale by Labor Day. Getting along with the guy who I live with is better than being at odds with him all the time but that doesn't mean I should change direction now. Does it?

"What are you talking about, dear boy? There has always been a you and Tack. Now it just happens to be a bit more tangible than back then, but it has always existed," she says, refilling my cup with tea. "I'm glad you aren't wearing that armor you paraded around in when you first came back. I think it's wonderful."

I know exactly what she's talking about but I'm too embarrassed to admit it. The truth is I feel a thousand pounds lighter than I have in a long time and I've smiled more the past few weeks than I have over the past few years.

She puts her hand over mine on the small tea table. "You have to see this thing with Tack through this time. Just be open to it. Don't run away."

"Toula, look, there is no thing with Tack," I say but it feels like more of a rehearsed response than a genuine thought. My plan has always been to have the inn ready for sale by Labor Day. Nothing has changed that. I'm having fun with Tack. It's a fling down memory lane not building a bridge to the future. Isn't it? I take a second to reset. This is Toula. She deserves my honest feelings. "We are getting closer again. That's true. His kid is great, really great, and the time alone is great, really great too but I don't want to name it or call it something that it isn't."

Maybe she's right. Maybe there is a thing with Tack.

"I understand, but just make sure you aren't acting out of fear."

"I'm a grown man. I'm not scared of anything," I say, bristling just a bit.

"Maybe the grown man isn't scared but the child Vince is always there. He's scared of suffering the rejection again from all those years ago. You're worried that if you say there is something between the two of you and it doesn't work out that it will hurt as much as before."

Toula chuckles softly and puts her hand on my arm. "Don't worry about that. It won't hurt as much as it did last time." She takes a sip of tea and then puts her cup down. "It will hurt *more*."

"Toula!" I say and steady myself on the chair by grabbing the armrests. She doesn't say anything; she just keeps looking at me with a knowing look in her eyes. She's letting me do the work myself and I can't stop the images from flooding my mind. It would be awful to leave right now. To give up what I have with Tack? Not feel his arms holding me when I wake up? Not stealing little glances during the busiest moment of dinner service that tell each other how proud we are of what we've built? And what about Jules? Could I really walk out on them? We've definitely established a connection. Could I handle not being able to be a part of their growing up? Doesn't it feel like Tack has already welcomed me into his heart and invited me to be part of their family?

She's right. The pain of leaving would hurt more this time.

"I should get back," I say and put my hand on her arm. I want her to know that I'm not angry in any way. I have a lot to think about.

"I know I push you but I also want you to know how thrilled I am to have you back." She gets up and gives me a hug. I don't have the guts to tell her the next time she sees me I might be saying goodbye again. As she wraps her arms around me she whispers in my ear, "You can do it. Remember, let the poem write itself."

I leave and I walk out onto the street and walk back down Main to the inn. I can't help thinking about what she said about staying open to things. What would it be like to see this thing through with Tack?

I don't know where it will go but she's right, maybe I need to let the poem write itself.

Chapter Twenty-Seven

Tack goes to culinary school in the mornings, and dinner service is getting busier each week. Whenever I can, I've been spending time with Tack and Jules. We went to Point Pleasant and tubed down the Delaware River watching the world float past us and found the best blueberry ice cream at a dairy in Solebury. We go to visit the goats at Uncle Kevin and Uncle Evan's whenever we are in range and even sometimes when we aren't because of Jules's love for Paul.

While the days are scenes from an affable sitcom, the nights are pure lust. We make out for hours on the couch while my laptop plays whatever Hulu show is on auto-play. I wake up with his mouth on my dick, hungrily waiting for my orgasm. The showers are just excuses to have sex standing up. I learn Tack's body in a way that I had only imagined. Years of fantasizing about him have actually created an endless menu of possibilities. We have been sucking and getting off multiple times a night pretty much every night for a few weeks now and I don't feel like we've scratched the surface of our passion.

We don't talk about the past or the future. We don't talk about what we mean to each other or where this is going. We just work hard and play harder.

Tack is working even harder than I am since he's also going to school in addition to making the inn a raging success. We're closed on Mondays since almost nothing is open in town and everyone seems to need a day to recuperate from the weekend.

I find Tack in the dining room alone, surrounded by books with his laptop open and his head on the table and the curtains drawn.

"Should I make you a double espresso?" I ask him and put my hands on his shoulders for a gentle massage.

"I'm not sure it would help," he grumbles, slowly raising his head. "It's not exhaustion. It's spreadsheets. I don't know how you keep the books for this place. It's impossible to keep track of everything and get the numbers to balance. I thought culinary school would just be about cooking. My Restaurant Operations class is kicking my ass. Again."

"Maybe I can help you," I say, walking over to the espresso machine. I try not to make a big deal out of it.

"I'll figure it out. It's just that the problems in the book don't make any sense. I've got to calculate a weekly cash flow statement for Cafe Paris," he says, clicking some keys on his laptop.

"Cafe Paris? Where is that, in Doylestown? Philly?"

"I wish. If it were a real place I could figure it out. It only exists in the mind of the author of this textbook. She has given us random numbers and inventory so none of it makes sense. They can't spend more on lemons than they do on meat. It makes the whole thing confusing."

"Hold on," I say. I run into the kitchen and grab my laptop and then come back to the dining room and grab the seat next to him. "Why don't I just walk you through our cash flow last week from the inn."

"I don't know if I'll understand it," he says. I put my hand on his thigh. Everyone sees Tack as the easygoing, handsome farm boy who never has to work at anything. I know Tack works hard at keeping up that appearance so when he is able to show me that he is unsure about something it's powerful. He's revealing a part of himself that no one else gets to see and it makes me feel even closer to him.

I start showing him each line in the cash flow and explaining how each part relates to an actual part of our operations so it makes more sense. The numbers are pretty simple and I know he understands them. It's the abstract nature of a textbook assignment that makes it confusing. I go over our beverage budget and then I look at the produce and dairy and other perishable goods the inn needs to create his menus. Then suddenly it clicks. I look at his face and I can see it all coming together.

"So that means the net change in cash from this week to the next should be…" He pauses for a moment then clicks a few keys. "That!" he says, pointing to a cell on the spreadsheet with the exact right number.

"Exactly!" I say. My phone rings and I look down at it. It's Barry. I can almost feel the blood drain from my cheeks down to my feet. I've been in complete denial about Barry and the deal that's brewing. Barry is relentless. It's what makes him so good at closing deals. I can't avoid him forever.

Tack sees me look at my phone and says, "You can go respond to that if you need to."

"It's not important," I say and shut off my phone completely. I sit down next to Tack but this time I'm physically much closer. Our thighs are touching but I stay focused on reviewing his computation.

"Excellent," I say. "It's perfect. This is exactly right."

"Thank you," he says but then his excitement gives way to a quietness. "No, really," he says. "You never made me feel stupid when I didn't understand something."

"Good, I want you to feel confident," I say and put my hand on his shoulder but this time my touch is not as gentle.

He looks at me and I take the opportunity to show him how I feel by moving my face next to his lips and kissing him slower than local honey moves downhill. My mouth opens to his and my tongue enters his mouth, searching for his, and when I find it our mouths open deeper and I feel even more connected to him. These long kisses have become as regular as our bread deliveries but much more exciting.

I look up from the kiss quickly just to make sure the shutters are closed in the dining room and then I stand him up, my mouth still on his. I grab for his pants, start undoing the fly and strip off all of his clothes in a matter of seconds. He goes to unbutton my shirt but I only let him get halfway down.

"No, I want to look at you." I'm fully dressed. Tack is completely naked. The power dynamic is raw and off-kilter and it makes me so hard. I want to just unzip my pants and see what it feels like to be inside him like this. I want him totally naked and vulnerable while I pound him in my shirt and pants. I approach him to find out when I hear loud knocking at the kitchen door.

"Anita?" Tack asks.

"It's Monday and she has a key," I remind him. The potential orgasm is affecting his thinking.

"The only person who should be knocking on your back door is me," he says and moves his fingers between my thighs right to my ass. "I'll go answer the door," he says, retreating from my ass.

"No, you study and stay naked. I'll take care of whoever it is." I button my shirt quickly and walk into the kitchen. I check myself once in the mirror to make sure nothing is hanging out that shouldn't be.

"Serilda," I say as soon as I open the door. "How nice to see you again." They are wearing a pair of lavender slacks and a floral blouse with multiple gold chains around their neck. "Stunning as always. I trust the LGBTQ Historical Society is having a good summer after the luncheon here Memorial Day weekend?"

"I know you're just flattering me but the ears hear the compliments just the same. Came by to discuss a little business with you but I must say I am quite disturbed by what I have seen." They raise their perfectly manicured eyebrows at me. Oh no. Did I miss a set of shutters? Did I just let the entire town see me strip Tack naked in the dining room?

"What did you see?" I ask, unable to hide a warble in my voice.

"Actually, it's what I didn't see."

"Excuse me?"

"What happened to the pride flags? They are a symbol of our community and let everyone know this is a safe place."

"Oh, yes," I say, relieved. "Those. Yes, I understand. The ones that were left behind by the previous owner were faded and, frankly, our community deserves better." The words come into my head like a sales pitch but by the time they are out of my mouth they don't feel that way at all. They feel like the truth. Maybe I should let the rainbow fly. Why not?

"I'm glad to hear it." They sit and then open a small notebook. "The historical society would like to host our fall luncheon at The Hideaway. Everyone is talking about how well you and Tack are doing."

I look over at the kitchen door and think about Tack's nearly naked body on the other side and how even a few seconds away from him is beginning to feel like too long.

"It's a bit of a bigger function than the one we had on the books when you took over the inn because it coincides with the High Heels Race. Local shopkeepers and officials race down Ferry Street in various forms of drag carrying a pumpkin. It's a fundraiser. Our community has found a home in this town for many, many decades. I know young people aren't always aware of the fact that they aren't the first person to fight the battle or that those before them have helped pave the way."

"I am aware," I say.

I think about meeting Toula all those years ago and how her kindness helped me do well in my classes despite all the tormenting. She recognized me in a way no one at school did. I know New Hope wasn't able to always protect me and those moments hardened me but the truth is without all the other good ones, like being in the bookstore, I wouldn't have survived.

"Let me be frank," they say, their tone changing from pleasant formality to familiar realness. "We ain't got a lot of money and the inn has always given us a steep discount. Are you gonna keep helping us?"

My first instinct is to say yes, of course, I would be happy to, but this response shocks me. When I hosted them in the spring I did it because it was already on the books and even though the profit was small I needed to show some money coming in. I told myself it was the last time I would be giving discounts and that I would be focused on making money not giving things away. But I want to help Serilda. What happened to my killer instincts?

"You are a very hard person to say no to," I tell them.

"I know. It's by design. I'm assuming that is a yes."

"Let me get the reservation book," I say, implying that a significant discount is in their future.

"Thank you, Vincent," they say, opening up a calendar from their purse.

"When is the event?"

"It's always the last Saturday in October."

"October?" I ask like they just said it was in the year 2050.

"Yes, I hope I'm not too late. Are you already booked?"

Booked? I had planned to be back in New York by Labor Day and lately I've been wondering about moving that deadline, but October? Even if the contract took longer than expected I thought I would close on a sale with Fun-Tyme before October. Then I remember the night after the reopening and Tack telling me that Jules wants the three of us to be a s'more. Sure, I briefly fantasized about going to the Halloween party as a—the word resists being summoned in my mind but then suddenly bursts through—*family*. But it didn't seem like it could be a reality. Now I can't help seeing the three of us dressed in brown and tan costumes that we need to explain to everyone we meet. An inside joke that makes the three of us laugh harder each time we have to explain it.

I remember my conversation with Toula. I can hear her reminding me that the pain will be worse this time. When I left New Hope last time I didn't know what I wanted. I was just a kid. But now I know exactly what I want and Toula is right—living a life alone without Tack and Jules would be miserable.

I don't want to sell to FunTyme or anyone else. I want to stay put and protect The Hideaway Inn.

I look over at the door to the dining room. I wonder if Tack is still naked. Still waiting for me. It feels like we have been waiting for each other forever but maybe the wait is finally over. My heart is so full of love for Tack right now that I think it might bust right out of my chest. I want to be with him and not just for the summer, for always. I want to be with him right here, working and loving together.

"Vincent? Are you available?" they ask, snapping me out of my pleasant daydream.

"Oh, I'm sorry. I was just clearing out a few things on the calendar to make sure we are available. I will most certainly be here," I say and turn to the correct page in the reservation book. "I'm putting you in for the last weekend in October. I will be at the door happy to see you and everyone in the LGBTQ Historical Society the day of the event."

"That's wonderful. I'll email you with details. Goodbye, Vincent." They put their hand on the door and then stop. "Oh, and tell Tack that if he wants to spy on your business meetings from the dining room he should at least put on a shirt."

They leave and I look over at the window in the door to the dining room. Tack's taut naked torso quickly darts away and I run through the door after him, ready to let the poem finally write itself.

Chapter Twenty-Eight

Tack

"Read it again. Start with the part that goes Chef O'Leary is the 'boss of flavor' but this time slow down and really put some feeling behind each word."

Vince has his phone in his hand and he's next to me in bed in his room which has slowly become *our* room over the past few weeks or so. His hairy legs are entwined with my smooth legs as he reads a customer review. We haven't been open long enough to have a ton of reviews but there are a few and they are pretty over the top.

The restaurant operated at a mad pace tonight— organized chaos that felt like being plugged into a power circuit. Every shake of a saucepan or sprinkle of a garnish felt like it was guided by intuition. The orders kept coming in and I had to keep a running tally in my head of everything that needed to be done and when. Every now and then I would glance over at Clayton as he brought in plates from the dining room and make sure they were empty. I swear a few looked like they were licked clean.

It was so busy I barely spoke to Vince but that doesn't mean we weren't connected the whole night. He spent most of the evening in the dining room with Anita, making sure each guest was enjoying their meal. Occasionally when the door swung open I would catch a glimpse of him listening to a customer or shaking someone's hand. My heart would swell with pride. But when he entered the kitchen and our eyes connected there was this understanding between us that we were working together, as a team. We had different tasks in front of us but each complemented the other.

It feels amazing to be appreciated in this way for something that I learned to do. I've always been told I'm handsome or I have pretty eyes or a sexy smile. That's nice. I mean, that feels good too but that's just winning the genetic lottery. This is different. This is being appreciated for something that's really a part of me.

I rub Vince's legs with my toes and he puts his arm around me as he reads the next. "'The summer gazpacho made with local heirloom tomatoes is Ah-MAZE-ing!'" he says. "That's how Chuckles456 wrote the word, just so you know. Then she says, 'It was a hot August day when we ordered the chilled soup and it was the perfect blend of cooling and zesty. I LOVED IT!!!' That is three exclamation points and all caps." I can tell he is trying to do his best dramatic interpretation but he refuses to let his voice rise into his upper register. I wish he would relax more with me, really trust me enough to be himself. But we're getting there and with each part of himself that he shares, I feel closer to him.

He reads one of my favorite lines and it's almost as good as hearing him moan when I'm about to make him come. I look at him reading and I can tell he is not only happy that the inn is doing well but he's proud of me and I think that is the best feeling of all.

"These are really great reviews. Anita and I should set up a media event," he says, pushing his finger across his phone to scroll through them.

"What do you mean?"

"Invite some big papers like *The Philadelphia Inquirer* or *The New York Times* and host a meal, maybe you do a cooking demonstration. Would help us get some press."

"If you think it would help, sure," I say. He takes his hand and softly moves it over my shoulder. It's so gentle and soft like he is barely making contact but that makes it that much more intense. Then he moves his hand off me.

"Oh, wait a minute, wait a minute," he says, sitting up in bed. "Who is this YoungBuck2525?"

"I have no idea," I say.

"Well, this YoungBuck on Yelp certainly knows who you are. Listen to this. 'It's no surprise that Tack's food is as delicious as he is. His ancho chile tamales with local goat cheese and artisanal honey were hot, spicy and perfectly golden just like the chef.'"

"No, it does not say that," I say, suddenly feeling bashful.

"It most certainly does." Vince holds his phone up to show me.

"Well, what can I say? I guess there are parts of me that are more golden than others." I roll over and show him my ass which is significantly paler than the rest of my body after a few days of playing shirtless with Jules by the river. I know the tan line looks sexy and I don't mind showing it off for Vince.

"You're such a tease." Vince sits up and grabs my forearms with his hands, pulling me up to him.

"You think so?" I say, lowering my chin and looking up at him.

"I do," he says, moving his mouth a breath away from mine. "I do," he repeats and then kisses me like the starter pistol of a race. But we aren't in any hurry. I move my lips down from his mouth, over the thick stubble on his chin and throat with gentle kisses that eventually reach all the way down to his neck. He moans deeply so I know I'm doing a good job. The hair on his body starts just beneath his shoulders on the front so it's almost like a knight's breastplate but covered in this thick fur that I have to admit turns me on more than I thought something could. I start kissing him at the top of his chest, switching between kissing, licking and playful nibble. I move my head lower and decide to take an express route past his very compelling nipples and down to his dick. I'm just at his waist when he stops me gently with his hand. I look up, willing to do whatever he wants.

"It's my turn," he says. Without skipping a beat his mouth goes right for my cock and starts sucking. I go to put my hands on his head or play with his nipples and he stops me. His force is more significant in his touch. This isn't the gentle brush of his hand. This energy says that he is in charge and I don't mind letting him.

His mouth gets faster and then slower on my cock. He's an expert at making me feel a range of sexual experiences. I can't help but reach out for him again and this time he takes my dick out of his mouth but keeps his face right next to it. He looks up at me and says, "Your only job right now is to sit back and enjoy this."

"I just want to…" I'm about to tell him some of the nasty things I want to do and but the pleasure I am experiencing takes over. I do as I'm told and lie on my back. His mouth and his hands are focused on my cock. The connection between his mouth and my dick is the only thing that exists in the world in that moment. It's incredibly hot and makes me want to shoot but I want to feel him as I orgasm.

I go to touch him and he pushes my hand away, exerting his role as Dom. I like to play this way sometimes, I guess, but right now I want to just touch him, feel him, let him know that he is sending me into a state of uncontrollable…

He suddenly goes for it, working my shaft so intensely that I have absolutely no control over the experience.

"Vince, yes, yes, yes," I scream from a place deep inside me.

I shoot hard into his mouth like bullets at a firing range that are many times stronger than they need to be to pierce their paper targets.

I look down and he is smiling and I can see his arm ricocheting as he finishes himself off. He shoots his load all over the floor next to the bed while our eyes stay focused on each other, conscious of the fact that we are sharing this moment together. Vince looks me up and down and a deep smile crosses his face. It's clear he is proud of what he has done.

He lies next to me on the bed and I put my arms around him. Immediately I start playing with the hair on his chest. I stroke it calmly and feel his breathing become deeper and more relaxed. I fall asleep next to him and dream about the key chain I lost years ago. I had carried that key chain around for years, rubbing the smooth surface with my fingers whenever I was stressed and nervous. It was a part of me but one day it was suddenly gone. I got new keys for my truck but I never found the key chain. Tonight, in my dream, I see it. Dangling just behind Axel's steering wheel is the smooth glass marble key chain with blue and brown swirls that I thought I'd never see again. I reach out for it assuming it will disappear like vapor but it doesn't. It's right there in my hand, exactly where it should be.

Chapter Twenty-Nine

"The food editor at *Philadelphia Magazine* and the editor of *Edible Philly* both confirmed. Still waiting on a few of the New York people," Anita tells me at our afternoon meeting between cafe and dinner service. After a day of rain the sun has made a spectacular return so we meet on the deck of the inn and try to focus on work and not watch the water and occasional boat or tuber float past.

Even though the media event is scheduled for just a week or so before Labor Day, Tack and Anita were able to score a full roster of some big names. I review the final list and see that some of the smaller gay and lesbian bloggers and local papers have already confirmed.

"Excellent, Anita, glad to see so many queer voices on this list," I say.

"Look at you embracing the community," she says, teasing me. "What happened to the guy who took down the old pride flags?" she asks, wheeling over to the other side of the deck to cross-check the list of attendees.

"I told you already. They were faded, old and falling apart."

"I hope you aren't talking about my peach upside-down cake?" Tack asks as he joins us on the deck.

"How did your big final in Restaurant Operations go this morning?" I'm hoping the big smile on his face is an indication.

"I never thought I'd be able to pass this class but I have to say I felt good about it this morning. None of the questions stumped me and when I got to the cash flow statement it all made sense."

"That's great," Anita says then she wheels over to where Tack and I are standing. "I have to make a deposit at the bank but I think we are all set for tomorrow." She looks us both up and down. "You make sure those dimples are firmly in place, Tack, and a few extra minutes with your beloved kettle bells wouldn't kill you, Vince."

"Yes, ma'am," I say, flexing my bicep to show her the goods and, if I'm being honest, to turn Tack on also.

"Does nothing for me," she says flatly. "But I know eye candy when I see it and you two are a Hershey bar and a bag of Skittles," she says, rolling down the ramp to the street.

"Wait," Tack says, calling after. "Which one is the Skittles?" Anita ignores him and continues on her errand.

"Well, obviously, I'm the Hershey bar. Dark, thick, melts in your mouth." I stand up and flex my muscles again.

"Take a breather, Candyman," he tells me. "Actually, stay seated. I want to give you something."

"Sure," I say, assuming he is going to be on his knees presenting me with his mouth but instead he runs back into the building and returns holding the most hideously wrapped package I have ever seen in my entire life.

"This is for you," he says.

"It looks like it broke off a rogue pride float," I say, examining the explosion of ribbons that decorate the box.

"Yeah, I kind of went overboard but I wanted to get you something to thank you for helping me with my class. I couldn't have done it without you."

"Of course you could have, but thanks. I have no idea what this could be," I say as I begin to tear through the wrapping. Once most of it is gone and I open the shoebox I see...shoes. But not oxfords or wingtips or even penny loafers. I pull out a pair of the largest red patent leather pumps that I have ever seen.

"I hope they fit," Tack says as I try to figure out who the hell he intends these for.

"Fit who? Me?"

I'm a smart guy. But with every synapse firing I cannot figure out what would make Tack think I would want a pair of high-heeled shoes. I wear suits and jockstraps and belts. The things people who identify as male wear. I don't dress up in women's clothes and I've never given him any indication that I want to do drag in any way.

"Try them on," he says.

"I'm not trying them on." I push the box away from me

like a plate of seafood that has gone bad. I'll just pretend this was a gag gift that went sideways.

"You'll never learn to run in them if you don't start practicing," he says and takes them out of the box. He puts them on his hands and mimics running.

"Tack, what the serious fuck are you talking about?"

He laughs but he is the only one in on the joke. "I take it you don't remember how New Hope celebrates fall."

"No, I don't," I say plainly.

"All of the business owners and community leaders race down Main Street in high heels carrying a pumpkin. The first person across the finish line gets to keep the trophy for the year. Well, it's actually not a trophy. It's a rubber chicken dressed as Joan Collins in *Dynasty* but same idea as a trophy. I thought you would remember," he says. Serilda had definitely described the event, come to think.

"Tack, I think that's a great fundraiser but not for me. We can donate food or space or whatever but I'm not going in drag." I respect anyone who needs to express their gender in any way they want. It's great and I'd fight hard for anyone's right to do it, but I've done my share of expressing. For me the scars from it are too deep to ever fade completely. I'm not the kid who got beat up for wearing eyeliner but I won't ever let myself be that vulnerable again. It's a line I won't cross. I can't. Not even for Tack. I put the lid back on the box. "Just return them."

"What's the big deal? Everyone participates and has a great time. Mario Luis, the fire chief, does it. His wife makes a dress for him that looks like a dalmatian every year. It's hysterical."

"Well, maybe I've had my fill of being laughed at in this town. So thanks, but no thanks." I'm growing more frustrated by the second. I can feel the blood racing through my heart building toward a panic but I try to keep it under the surface.

"No one would be laughing at you. They would be laughing with you."

The laughter sounds the same to me. "No thanks, I said."

"Vince, come on. What are you so scared of?"

"I'm not scared of anything," I say, making sure I sound confident and in charge. I thought I was done covering up my deeper feelings with bravado but the process comes back so effortlessly I wonder if I've only taken a hiatus.

"You can't be yourself for one day? For one race down Main Street. It's a charity fundraiser." He takes the rainbow wrapping paper and starts crumpling it into small balls.

I know I've been slipping lately, letting my guard down around him and no one is more surprised about that than I am. Being with him has an effect on me that makes me *want* to slip. But he's hammering at the very foundation of who I have worked so hard to become and I don't like it. "Enough, Tack. Leave it alone, please. Just accept that I don't want to do it," I say but the look in his eyes tells me he is in too deep. He's as hurt and confused as I am.

"I thought you could be yourself and not care what anyone else thinks. Apparently you're more interested in this person you created, this hyper-masculine stand-in for some action movie, rather than the guy who I have been falling…"

He stops.

I don't say anything. I wait for him to finish. I need to hear him say it in this moment. Maybe he's about to, maybe not, but the waiting and the silence are too much for me to bear. I find a way out.

"Tomorrow is a big day," I say in my best calm-neutral. "Let's just get through the dinner service and the media event," I say as calmly as I can. I'm taking big breaths through my nose to stop from crying and screaming.

"Fine," he says, grabbing the box from the table and stomping off the deck like a child.

I sit down at the table and try to focus my thoughts. But I can't help asking myself—if I've spent so long making sure there isn't anything in the world I'm afraid of then why am I sitting alone with my head in my hands feeling so scared?

Chapter Thirty

Tack

I was sure by the time I started prepping dinner service I would have forgotten about my fight with Vince but when I get to the kitchen it's still on my mind. It's not about him rejecting the present. That's not the point. It's the fact that Vince still feels he can't be himself around me and that maybe he never will.

I grab the sharpening stone I borrowed from a restaurant down the street where the sous chef is an alum of my cooking school. I run the stone under some cool water and plan to take my frustration out on the knives at The Hideaway. Our kitchen seems to be a refuge for the dullest, oldest knives in Pennsylvania. For a second I miss the knife set I sold at the beginning of the summer but then I think about how happy Jules is at the Chapman Creek camp and I don't mind taking some time each week to sharpen dull spatulas, masquerading as knives, at the inn. The repetitive motion of the blades helps me not think about Vince.

Doesn't Vince see that I want to build something with him here? Nothing has ever felt as right as being with him does. I never thought he would return. I thought that door was closed but if it's going to open again it needs to be real. It can't be based on some idea Vince has of himself because the whole thing will fall apart again and I know I won't be able to handle that.

I grab the next knife and slowly run the blade against the stone, feeling the sleek surface of the metal connect with the grit of the stone—two opposites coming together to make something stronger.

There is a knock at the door but I don't get up. I just yell, "Come in," and stay focused on my work. A woman in a blue suit carrying a briefcase walks in. I've never seen her before.

"I'm looking for Mr. Vincent Amato. He is the owner, correct?"

"Yes, but he's not here. I'm the chef. Can I help you?"

"I did want to see him in person to go over the numbers with him."

"Is this about a supplier? We only use local vendors."

"Not for long," she says and lets out an irritated sigh. "I have a meeting in Philly I have to make. I'm passing through on my way from New York and wanted to go over some of this to expedite the sale. I know Mr. Amato is eager to unload this place."

"Unload?" I can feel the blood drain from my face. This must be some kind of mistake. "I didn't know the inn was for sale."

"Everything is always for sale." She laughs like she is about to purchase a sack of dalmatians. "Mr. Amato knew what he was doing when he bought this place. Great location. The interior is bit shabby but that can all be torn out. Your boss does have an eye for flipping properties."

"Flipping properties?" I echo. I can hear the words coming out of my mouth like someone else is saying them. It feels like I'm trying to stop something from happening even though the spring is already wound.

"Oh sorry, shop talk. It means taking an old, worn-out property nobody wants and selling it for a profit."

"I know what it means," I tell her sharply but the words *old, worn-out* and *nobody wants* ring so loudly in my ear I can barely see straight. "You mean he just bought this place to flip? He had no intention of staying in New Hope?" I ask, swallowing hard.

"No way. From what I've heard, once he signs this contract he'll be out of here before the ink is dry." She opens her briefcase and takes out a large envelope.

My vision blurs and my head starts to pound. Vince never had any intention of staying with me. We were never building anything together. It was never the two of us turning the place around. I can't believe I thought we were a team. I've been planning on building a life with him and he's been thinking about the tax liability of a quick sale. How could I have been so stupid?

Then the bottom really drops out.

Jules has grown so close to Vince this summer. How am I going to tell my child that the one man who made their father feel complete was only using him? The very thought of having that conversation with Jules makes me almost vomit.

"I'm sure your boss will be very pleased with the offer from FunTyme," she says, completely unaware that she has just destroyed me.

"FunTyme?" I know that name from culinary school. They have a terrible reputation in the hospitality business. I didn't think this news could get any worse. "You guys bought out all the small taco shops at the beaches around San Diego. Turned them into TacoTyme. Right?"

"Yes! You heard about that deal? I worked on that. We bought those shacks for pennies on the dollar. A lot of those shacks were just teardowns. It was cheaper to build prefab." She looks at her watch. "I have to run." She drops the envelope on the table next to me. "Can you make sure Vincent gets this offer? I think he'll be pleased with the number. This is going to make a fabulous RiverTyme property." She walks out the door.

I look down at the sharpening stone. I'm trying to remain calm and focus on what's in front of me even though my world is falling apart. All the water that provided lubricant for the blade has dried out. I shouldn't, but I grab the next knife, hold it to the dry stone and push it against the surface hoping the blade won't resist the stone. I use too much force and the knife slips. The blade slices the side of my finger. It's only a superficial slice but I try to focus on the physical pain instead of letting my mind take in what I've just heard. A tear falls onto the cut sending an acute sting through my hand. My finger is fine but the damage is worse than I thought.

Chapter Thirty-One

After our fight about the high heels, I run some errands and by the time I'm back dinner service has started. We manage to make it through the entire night without speaking a word to each other. I work on some last-minute details for the media event the next day while he finishes in the kitchen but by the time I get up to the apartment he has turned out the lights and his door is shut. Maybe I overreacted a bit, but I was hoping we could talk about it. Tack's closed door shows me that he has zero interest in working this out.

The next day by the time I'm up he's out of the apartment. As I'm getting dressed I keep thinking I hear him come up the stairs and my heart races. I'm disappointed when I don't see his face at the doorway.

By the time I get downstairs Anita has everything set up perfectly for the media event. As soon as she sees me she turns towards the kitchen door and yells out. "Tack, he's down you can go up now." Tack darts through the kitchen up the stairs without so much as a nod in my direction.

I know we had an argument but why is he completely shutting me out? He can't be that nervous about the media event. He's a natural in front of people.

"I don't have time to referee with you boys today. Now, I need you to go over these remarks and review the RSVP list." Anita hands me some notecards and a folder with papers in it.

"Fine," I say like a petulant child and go to the dining room to review the material. I push through the kitchen door and I'm struck by how beautiful the place looks. I hadn't noticed the effect because it had been incremental but in this moment I'm able to see how the place has transformed. When I first arrived I wanted to just gut the place and make it modern rustic but with Anita and Tack whispering in my ear to keep the traditional charm of the place I gave in and I have to admit I'm glad I did. The place is not grand or stunning but it's comfortable and charming. I can imagine making this place a thriving business with Tack. We finally open up the rooms and maybe expand the owner's suite so there is more room for Jules when they come to stay and a place for them to hang out with their friends. Life on the river might not be bad at all.

"Out. Out!" Anita says, rolling through the door. I've been so lost in my daydream that I haven't paid attention to the time. "I've spent hours making everything perfect in here. I don't need you messing it up. Tack's ready in the kitchen." I get up to join him.

"Who's here?" I ask.

"A few of the city papers. One of the queer food bloggers we wanted and a small local paper that has a big following."

"Great," I say. "Is Tack ready?"

"Yes. I want you two to put on your happy faces. He's all set to do a cooking demo in the kitchen."

Tack walks into the dining room looking perfect. I never had a thing for chef aprons before but this summer has changed that. The white fabric clings to him in just the right places and makes his golden skin look even more so next to the crisp cotton.

"Are we all set?" he asks, making sure his eyes don't connect with mine.

"I believe so," I respond, echoing his flat tone.

"Let's get this show started, Mr. Amato. After all, time is money," Tack says and quickly enters the kitchen.

Something is going on. This isn't about a stupid pair of shoes. I want to pull Tack aside but when I follow him into the kitchen, Anita has everyone seated around his open workstation and Tack has started.

"Thank you all for coming," Tack says to the small crowd. His voice lacks its usual charm and playful cadence. "Today I'm planning to demo a roasted vegetable frittata using local and organic ingredients."

The reporters murmur their approval and this is my cue to talk about the local suppliers.

"Thanks, Tack. We've worked hard at The Hideaway Inn to develop relationships with the community that will benefit everyone. Most of all, our customers, who get delicious food created by our wonderful chef."

"Thanks, Vince," Tack says stiffly and continues. He loosens up during the actual demo since he is in his element. He cracks eggs, chops vegetables and shows off just enough to capture everyone's attention. The reporters take notes and a few of them take pictures. I'm sure Tack will look as delicious as the food. Before Anita ushers everyone into the dining room for brunch, I ask if anyone has any questions.

There are a few about the ingredients and then a few about Tack's culinary background and then the woman from the queer blog raises her hand. "I have a question for Vince."

"Go ahead," I say.

"There was a rumor earlier in the summer that The Hideaway was being eyed by a real estate developer that wanted to put a chain in this space. Is that true?"

I give a short laugh to shift the mood. "That was just a rumor. I'm the owner and I can tell you there is no hostile takeover looming."

"May I say something, Mr. Amato?" Tack asks. I nod hesitantly. Any joy he may have exhibited during the demonstration has completely evaporated. "I may just be the chef but with the help of Mr. Amato, I've learned a thing or two about business recently."

For a second I think he is going to publicly thank me for helping him with his Restaurant Operations class but one look at the sharp squint of his blue-gray eyes and I know that's not what he's going to say.

"The thing about a hostile takeover is that it might not be hostile at all. It might seem sweet and kind and say all the right things. It might make you think that you can finally relax. That everything is going to work out. But then..." He grabs a cleaver and takes a random carrot from his prep area and lowers the blade down. "You find out you've been on the chopping block all along." One half of the now severed carrot rolls off the cutting board on to the floor.

I need to get everyone out of the kitchen and have this out with Tack. "That ends our demonstration, everyone. Please join us in the dining room." I open the kitchen door and usher everyone through as quickly as possible.

We're alone in the kitchen and I lay into him. "What was that? Are you rehearsing a scene from *Whatever Happened to Baby Jane*? Are you still mad at me from yesterday?" My voice is gentle and reconciliatory, trying to get him to look at me. "Look, I'm sorry. We're trying to build something together here and we're not always going to get it right."

"Oh, are we? Is that what's happening? You and me? We are trying to build something? Did you think I would just go along with your whole scheme? The dumb farm boy tricked by the fancy rich real estate tycoon?"

"What are you talking about?"

He walks over to the desk behind the kitchen demo area and opens a drawer to pull out an envelope. "This was hand delivered for you yesterday. It's an offer to buy the inn. The woman who delivered thought this place would make, and I quote, 'a fabulous RiverTyme property.'"

The look on Tack's face is so simultaneously sad and angry, I can barely meet his eyes. Why didn't I return

Barry's calls and tell him I didn't want to sell? I know he kept leaving messages and I should have told him I wasn't interested anymore. I should have calculated that FunTyme would be ready to make offers by now and told Barry that The Hideaway is *not* for sale. More importantly, why didn't I tell Tack about this when I changed my mind?

"Let me explain," I plead.

"Explain what? I'm not that stupid. I get it. You pump some life into this place and then sell it to the highest bidder. You had no intention of staying around here. You just came here to flip this place. Fuck the local chef while you're at it. You don't care about me or this place or this town. You just want to turn a profit. How could you betray me like this? Lead me on?"

"I haven't betrayed you. Yes, I was planning to flip the place when I got here but that was in May. Months ago. That was before..."

I stop.

I don't tell him that was before I fell in love with him. Before I started fantasizing about helping him raise Jules? Before I thought about making a family? Before. Before. I feel myself getting lost in a fantasy that maybe never really had any hope of coming true.

"Months ago? Vince, that's worse. Was it all just part of putting together an attractive package for FunTyme? Was 'local chef' just one of the items on the balance sheet to you?"

Tack takes the envelope he's been holding and throws it on the table like it's toxic waste.

"I don't want to sell. I'm *not* selling the inn," I say.

"Are you sure? You haven't even looked at the offer. Might be exactly the number to change your mind. That's what matters to you in the end—profit, not people. Vinny was a great kid but Vince turns out to be a real asshole."

I don't say anything. Maybe he's right.

"I thought this time would be different with us. I have worked so hard to be with you. To show you who I am now, to share myself and my family with you."

"I know that. I've loved that. I love that. I love being with you and Jules."

"Poor Jules. You were working on this deal all summer? You knew about it during the Fourth of July, when we went tubing, at every visit to the farm."

"I knew about it, yes. But Tack—"

"It's not even about the deal at this point. The people here will never let a chain move in. I know them. It's about you, Vince. I can't trust you."

The words hit me like darts dipped in acid. I feel the walls closing in and my options vanishing. I put my hand on the table to steady myself.

"Tack, please, you can't mean that. How could you say that?" Everything I was feeling, everything I felt with him was real. He has to know that. He has to have felt that.

"Well, you do have an envelope with a deal in it in front of you that you've told me nothing about." He throws his open palm out toward the document. I stare at it. Two feet in front of me are both my future and my past. But I can't seem to wrap my mind around which is which in this moment. If Tack can't trust me what's the point in staying here? If he doesn't believe in us then what we have—or rather, what we had—isn't real.

I realize that I screwed up here but regardless the rejection from Tack feels like a muscle memory rising from my core.

"I can't go through this again," I say and put my hand on the envelope.

"You're taking the deal?" he asks, spitting out each word like poison. I don't know what to do exactly.

"Is that what you want me to do?"

"Is that what you want to do?"

It's not the answer I was hoping for. If Tack wanted me to stay he would have said so. He's been lashing out with honesty all day. Why would he stop now? I grab the envelope from the table and hold it in my hand, giving him one last chance to stop me from leaving.

"Go ahead, run away. That's what you did last time. I should have known that you would do it again. You're this big tough guy who came back here to teach everyone a lesson about how successful you are now. I got it. Lesson learned. You're done here." The passion that was in his eyes just a few days ago has been replaced with a steely glare.

He's fucking right and the realization knocks the wind out of me.

Everything I thought I was doing to protect myself was actually destroying what I tried to build. Tack could never want to be with someone who has deceived him, never mind want Jules to be around someone as insensitive as I've been. My insides start to crumble like a cave about to collapse in on itself. How could I have been so stupid, so pigheaded, so wrong about *everything*?

I can't be with Tack a second longer. I turn away from him completely defeated and walk out of the kitchen unable to look back.

Chapter Thirty-Two

Tack

"There's nothing to say," I tell Evie again and wipe the tears from my eyes. "He's leaving. He was always going to leave." I'd called to tell her I was going to be late to pick up Jules and she could hear something was wrong in my voice. Evie asked her aunt Rhoda to stay with Jules and then Evie came over and met me in a quiet spot on the bank of the river next to the playhouse.

"Evie, he never wanted to be here. He didn't really want to start a life with me. It was just a way to boost his profit. He's not the Vinny I remember."

Evie laughs gently. "And you aren't the same Tack."

"I guess that's true," I say and stare out at the muddy

water as it rushes past us. "Things were going so well, at least I thought they were. I wanted this to be our second chance. I disappointed him in school, I know that. First I sent him mixed messages and then when I couldn't take it I just blew him off and married you."

"Ouch!" Evie says. She turns away from me and faces the river. I'm a dirty bomb of emotional destruction today.

"That was a shitty thing to say. It wasn't like that. You know that. We had great times and I loved you. I still do."

"I know," she says, turning back. "I love you too and I'm grateful that we co-parent so well. I want you to find what I found with Ines." She puts her hand on my arm. She's always been so understanding with me.

"I know Jules needs that. They need to see both their parents in stable relationships." I want my kid to see that their dad is capable of that.

"It's not just for Jules, it's for you too. We both want *you* to be happy. Jules came home after tubing with you and Vince and would not stop talking about how much fun they had and how their dad was so happy and what a great time all three of you had together."

"I know it was great." The three of us went tubing down a gentle part of the Delaware on one of the swelter-ing hot days last week. We tied our tubes together so that no one would float away. I liked floating but I liked feel-ing connected to two of the most important people in my life even more.

I look out at the river. The water looks more brown than gray today and the level seems higher than usual. Even when I don't see it for days or weeks or when it floods or a drought reveals the hidden islands that rise to the surface, the river is always there, no matter what happens or what I do.

"I love him, Evie. I think I always have."

"I *know* you always have," she says gently. "Tack, I'd have to have worn a sack on my head to not see the looks you two gave to each other at school every time one of you thought the other wasn't looking. Maybe neither of you saw them, but I did. You two belong together, you always have. I wish you could both see it."

Suddenly it all makes sense. I need to make him *see* it. I know I can't sit down and talk with him face to face right now. Everything is too raw. Nothing will come out right. Maybe there is a way I can show him. I look out at the river and see a fallen tree branch sticking up out of the water. The obstacle does little to impede the water; the river always finds a way to flow, to get where it's going. I know exactly what I can do to make him understand.

"Evie, thank you." My head is already racing ahead figuring out the logistics of what I need to do. I'm walking away from her as fast as I can. I have to make it back to The Hideaway before Vince picks up his stuff and leaves for New York.

"Wait. Where are you going? What are you going to do?" she asks.

"Something I should have done a long time ago," I shout back to her as I run up the river walk back to the inn.

Chapter Thirty-Three

For many years, the Gramercy Park Hotel was my playground. The overstuffed leather chairs and dramatically lit potted palms were a background to a variety of hijinks. Usually when I walk into the lobby I'm met with a certain rush of excitement but today I only compare it to the quirky comfort of The Hideaway and feel a flutter in my heart. I really grew to love that place but it doesn't matter anymore. I screwed up the whole thing. It's time to pick up where I left off.

After I packed my bags at the inn, I waited for a car service to pick me up and take me back to New York. I opened the offer from FunTyme on the way into the city and the number was significantly higher than I could have expected but it doesn't make me any happier to have to take the deal. I called Barry to arrange a meeting to sign off on the contract immediately. I also told him I'd like to approach FunTyme about a full-time position in their New York office or one of their overseas branches. Anything to get me as far from New Hope as possible. Barry said he would float my name around and see what he could do. No matter how much I may want things to be different, there isn't anything keeping me in New Hope anymore.

"Mr. Amato, it's very good to see you here again." The concierge comes over to greet me with a smile that shows me he has got more than dinner reservations on his mind.

"Max, it's good to see you as well," I say, surveying the way his perfectly structured cheeks and lips are made even sexier by the slightly sunburnt edge of his nose.

"We didn't see you on Fire Island this summer. People are wondering where you've been," he says, grabbing my bag.

"Well, I took a little detour this year," I say, hoping my eyes don't reveal the fact that I'm lying my ass off. I didn't take a detour. I took a huge gamble and I lost.

"I'll be able to sneak away in about an hour." He looks from side to side and then comes within a few inches of me. "Would you like some company?" he whispers in my ear.

Max is a stunning guy, all muscle, and we've had some fun in the past. Usually I'd have this guy's legs in the air before the elevator doors have had a chance to close. He's my type—a total ten and ready to worship me exactly as I want.

Sex should be on the agenda; it's a great mind eraser. In the past I've used any number of hard-muscled studs to

diminish my stress or make a failed deal seem less important. Hooking up will prove that I never really had true
feelings for Tack.

Max gives me another devilish smile. I should tell him
to be at my door in fifty-nine minutes but I don't. I lie
and tell him I can't tonight because of a conference call. I
head upstairs alone.

I open the door to my suite. Usually the crisp white
sheets on the bed, the perfectly framed view of Gramercy
Park and the minimal decor make me feel powerful and
in control but I don't get that rush this time. Today it feels
cold and empty.

For a second I think about the fireplace at the inn and
the uneven walls that make it clear the place was built in
another century. I take a deep breath and push that thought
out of my head.

Barry isn't in until late tomorrow night so I just crawl
up into a ball on the bed and force myself to sleep.

I spend the next day trying to change gears by doing the
things I love doing in the city. I go for a run from Gramercy
over to Chelsea Piers and all the way down to Lower Manhattan, following the water down and back up on the east
side. Usually a long run makes me feel exhilarated but at
the end I'm exhausted. I grab a hot dog from Gray's Pa-
paya and undo all of that work but I can't help myself from
slathering the whole thing in mustard, ketchup and as much
sauerkraut as they will let me have. I end up taking only
a couple of bites before throwing the rest away. I never

thought I'd have a problem that a greasy hot dog couldn't ameliorate but I've completely lost my appetite.

Finally I go to the Museum of Modern Art to visit my old friend, Cézanne's *The Bather*, a painting I've sort of had a thing for since I first saw it as a teen.

The museum is crowded but I'm able to stand right in front of the masterpiece. A teenage boy painted in somber shades of blue stands at the edge of the water in his swimsuit with his hands on his hips. He looks down, avoiding eye contact with the observer. He is shy and unsure of himself but also present in his surroundings. He is almost naked but not in a sexual way. He is exposed but also without pretense, without a facade.

I used to identify with this boy so much. I used to think it was a portrait of me but now I have much more in common with the suits of armor a few dozen blocks uptown at the Met. I'm rarely vulnerable like the boy in the frame before me. I'm always wearing a shield that has been polished and maintained over the years but I wonder if there is still a boy underneath.

I used to think the painted boy was weak, like I was as a kid. But I realize now he isn't weak at all. Being a man isn't something you become or something you show people. I don't know what it is. I used to think it was the most important thing in the world. If I was a man, I could be safe. I wouldn't have my fate decided by the people around me. If I could be a man, in the way the world wanted me to be, maybe I would be worthy of love.

I always thought that was the thing that stopped Tack from being with me. *I wasn't worthy.* I thought he was embarrassed of me. I've spent my whole life trying to be worthy and now I don't even know what that is. What's worse, I don't think it even matters.

I think about Jules and their lack of interest in defining themselves. If I wasn't so worried all summer about showing Tack who I've become, maybe I'd have found a way to tell him the truth about everything. Maybe I would be at The Hideaway Inn right now sitting on the porch with both of them.

I take in the blues and greens of Cézanne's brushstrokes. I just stand in front of the painting like it's only me and the canvas and nothing else exists in the world. I study it not for the composition or use of color but for what it says to me privately.

"Sir, I think you may need this?" A frail woman with a walker says to me, pulling out a tissue from her sleeve.

"Excuse me?" I say, breaking the spell.

"Here," she says. "Take as many as you need." She gives me her compact package of tissues and walks away. I hold them in my hand and suddenly see a drop of water dampen the tissue waiting to be pulled from the pack. For a moment I think the ceiling at the museum has a leak but then I realize it's a tear. I've been standing in front of the painting crying and I didn't even know it.

Chapter Thirty-Four

After the museum I go back to my suite. I don't have the appetite for roaming the jungle like I used to. Instead, I fall asleep. My phone rings and wakes me from another nap. I look at my watch and see I have slept most of the evening away.

"Hey, Barry," I say, trying not to sound like I just woke up. This is the call I have been waiting for.

"Vince, how's it feel being back in the city? I bet you pounded every guy in a flannel shirt within a fifty-mile radius of that town." He laughs loudly into the phone.

"Something like that," I say, rolling over on the bed. I can't tell if I'm not in the mood for Barry's ribald humor or completely over it.

"I'm downstairs at the bar with a whiskey neat with your name on her. Get that sexy ass down here."

"Fuck you," I say in our usual jib-jab banter. "I'll be down in a few minutes."

When I get to the bar I see Barry talking to a sweet-faced bartender who can't be more than twenty-six—less than half Barry's age. I used to think Barry had so much power. He was so good at his job that businesses overlooked the fact that his personality was so overbearing.

"Good evening, sir. What can I get you?" the bartender asks me. I can't tell if he is grateful to have someone distract Barry.

"Hey, college boy. I've dropped enough tips here to pay your tuition for a year. I know Pretty Boy is…you know, pretty," Barry says, gesturing to me, "but don't forget who is greasing your tip jar." He isn't drunk but I can tell he has had enough to loosen him up even more than normal. I'm beginning to see how insecure Barry is underneath all his bravado—insecure and lonely.

"I think my friend already has one for me. Thank you," I say.

"Good to see you, buddy." Barry shakes my hand the way we were taught. He grabs my forearm, looks me in the eye and grips hard. This is how a man shows power in business. Usually my grip is like a vise but today I don't feel the need.

"I've got the contracts with me all signed and ready to go. I also have a bunch of ideas for managing the chain from New York and I've looked into FunTyme's foreign assets.

I thought I could run some of my ideas by you and you could get me in to see some of the key players this week."

"Slow down. First tell me about the guys you've been doing this summer. I bet there are some hot farm boys out in the middle of nowhere," he says and takes a swig of his drink. I close my eyes for a second and rub my temples to stop the phrase "hot farm boys" from entering my mind. There's only ever been one hot farm boy for me and I destroyed any chance of ever having that work out. I need to change the subject and focus on business.

"Actually, I've been working really hard. I haven't had time for much of that," I say.

"Yeah, right. Vince Amato the power top taking a break. No one is going to believe that."

"Well, they should," I say firmly but not harshly. I'm determined to change the subject. "I'd really like to talk about finding a position at FunTyme that would allow me to make a considerable contribution either in New York or at one of their abroad offices."

Barry takes the last swallow of his drink and pushes the empty glass away. "You won't let up. All business today, huh?" he says with a newfound soberness.

"Just want to make sure we are on the same page. I've always gotten my work out of the way before play."

Barry raises his eyebrows at me. "Well, not always, buddy."

"What's that supposed to mean?"

"Vince, look, everyone knows you have a reputation. You were found fucking in the conference room at your last job."

"I know," I say, looking down. That seems like a million years ago.

"Personally I think you are a total stud but that's hard to live down."

"Look, that's all in the past. How long do I have to pay the price for that? I made a mistake. It was all consensual. I'm ready to sell. I just want to be part of the package."

"I've got to be honest with you. I thought there might be some opportunity for you on this deal and I tried to push your name. I really did. I should have told you before you came back to the city but the truth is, they want the inn, they don't want you. I thought maybe Pete Squills would be on your side because I thought the two of you had a thing but he was one of the guys against you."

"What?" I know I have the skills to be a part of Fun-Tyme. I didn't know Pete was part of the management team. Then I remember ignoring his texts after he wouldn't get the hint that I didn't want our one-night stand to be anything more than that. "That asshole," I mutter.

"Yeah, well, he pretty much feels the same way." Barry moves his almost empty glass to his mouth.

So much for my big comeback.

"I'm sorry, buddy. It's not gonna happen. But look on the bright side. They want the inn. You'll make some nice coin on that deal."

I take the whiskey he ordered from me and down it without as much as a blink. "Do me a favor, Barry. When you go back to the management team tell Mr. Squills that I don't give a fuck if I never see him or his lousy toupee ever again." Barry looks surprised. "Come on, it looks like a Beanie Baby died on his head."

Andrew must overhear me because he laughs to himself as he wipes out a glass far away from Barry. I'm glad at least someone is laughing because I'm not. I walk out of the bar and head up to my room. But by the time the elevator reaches my floor my anger at Barry and the situation has turned to sadness. I was kidding myself to think I could just push the reset button. I can't really see myself prowling hotel bars with Barry when my heart is still in New Hope with Tack and his kid. I've replayed the past three months in my head over and over identifying dozens of moments where I could have told Tack how I really felt and confessed that my original plans had changed. I was so intent on showing him what a successful man I've become that I didn't bother to show him the rest of me. The part that needs his love more than anything else.

I walk into my room, head right to the minibar and twist off the tops of whatever booze I can find. I'm not a big drinker but this particular shit show calls for something to numb my brain. I'm not even close to being buzzed. I don't even get a glass. I want to down these little bottles immediately. I grab the first one, some fancy-assed vodka, and twist the top off but my grip is so overly tight that the little metal top cuts deep enough into my hand to make it bleed. At first it seems superficial but I quickly realize I should at least find a Band-Aid.

As I dig around in my suitcase for a bandage of some sort I feel something about the right size for my toiletries kit but the wrong shape. What is this? Like a magician pulling something out of a hat I grab the object to reveal a book.

I don't remember packing a book. I can tell from the back of it that it's quite old. When I turn it over I know exactly what it is. The shock of it knocks me out more than the entire contents of the minibar would be able to.

It all comes flooding back to me. I can see the steps by the school. I can see Tack walking past it. I can see leaves blowing over it and almost feel the rain that falls on it as the storm begins. In my hands is Baldwin's *The Fire Next Time*. This must be a copy.

But then I open it and I see my handwriting:

To Tack. From Vinny.

The blue ink is faded and I immediately remember how I practiced making a curly design on the V in my name before I signed the book. Right under the original inscription is a new one.

It says:

Vince, I'm sorry. No more masks. I love you. Tack. Page 43.

My hand scrambles into my pocket and I grab the packet of tissues the old woman gave me at the museum. I swear I'm going to camp out in front of that Cézanne to wait for her so I can thank her because my face is so covered in tears that I can't read the text of the book. I wipe away as many as I can, turn to page forty-three and read the underlined text: "Love takes off masks that we fear we cannot live without and know we cannot live within."

I always thought Tack left the book on the table under the trees and that the janitor or somebody went to throw it out the next day. Not only did he go back to get it but he kept it all these years.

I thought I was repeating the past but the past turns out not to be what I thought it was. I don't need to pay for the past and I don't need to be ruled by it. What I need to do is accept the past for what it was and allow the present to be what it needs to be.

Tack loves me. Tack has always loved me and his love makes me feel like I can be *The Bather*—vulnerable but this time safe.

Now I am full-out crying, something I haven't done in a very long time. I feel the tears melting away my mask and let it dissolve without the slightest sign of a fight.

Chapter Thirty-Five

"Are you sure this bus stops in New Hope?" I ask before boarding.

"Son, what do those lights above the windshield say?" The driver is in no mood.

"I want to make a hundred percent sure," I say.

The driver looks me up and down over the top of his glasses. "I guess you aren't so confident without your fancy suit and expensive shoes." I'm just wearing a T-shirt and a pair of old jeans. I was hoping the driver wouldn't remember me. I guess being an asshole makes you memorable.

"Sorry about all the attitude last time," I say. My voice comes out a bit higher and definitely more humble than usual. It's more sincere than polished but it feels comfortable in my throat.

"Uh-huh," the driver says.

"And can you tell me if this is an express to New Hope or the local."

"Express. You in a hurry?"

"Yeah, I've waited almost fifteen years for a happy ending and I can't wait a second longer."

"Well, in that case I'll try not to miss the exit." He cracks the smallest smile and I hop on the bus.

I'm not usually able to sleep on cars or planes but the last day has been so draining emotionally that I'm out as soon as we hit the highway.

"New Hope. Last stop New Hope," I hear the driver say as he honks the horn. I walk down the aisle and the driver says, "You almost missed it."

"Almost, but I'm awake now. I think I'm finally awake."

I step off the bus and it takes me a second to adjust to the sunlight. Main Street looks magical in late summer since the ancient oak trees create a lush canopy of green and the shops spill out on to the sidewalks with end of season sales. It used to feel like Manhattan was the center of the universe but I think I've found the center of my world. It's here. Maybe it's always been here and I never knew it. Or maybe this is something new. It doesn't matter. I just know I have to build my life in this place, with Tack.

When I open the door to The Hideaway, it's empty. I call out for Tack, Anita or even Clayton and no one is anywhere to be found. I grab my bag and pull out the tightly wrapped package of brand-new knives I bought at a culinary shop in Chelsea before boarding the bus. I dropped a small fortune on them but I wanted Tack to know I've been paying attention and show him I recognize his talent.

"Tack? Anita?" I call out. Have they all abandoned ship? Couldn't they at least stick it out a few more days? I see a Post-it note on the floor that must have fallen off the door. I bend over to pick it up and read it. "Anita—Had to go to Lambertville Urgent Care with Jules. Still no word from Vince. Tack."

I don't think.

I walk out of the inn and toward the bridge. The Lambertville Urgent Care is just on the outskirts of town. I start walking but as soon as I hit the bridge I get a sudden rush of adrenaline. I'm so worried that something might have happened to Jules that my entire body kicks into the next gear and I run the rest of the distance. Lambertville is a blur until I get to the entrance to the urgent care. "I'm looking for Tack O'Leary and his child, Jules. I'm a friend. A close friend of the family." I am covered in sweat and completely out of breath. The man at the desk probably thinks I need to be admitted.

The door to the treatment area swings open and I see Tack. He's talking to someone in scrubs but when the door swings again I see that person walking away and Tack turns towards me.

I push past the door and stand in front of him. His face is stained with tears but his eyes still sparkle with the essence that is Tack.

"I saw the note. How's Jules? What happened? Are they okay?" I ask. I grab Tack's forearms and we are face to face.

"What are you doing here? I thought you left for New

York," he says. The shock of seeing me is sinking in and we are locked together in a hold I'm not sure I ever want to break.

"I did. I came back. It's not important right now. How is Jules?"

"They're fine. They're going to be fine. They left with Evie in my truck about ten minutes ago. I just finished the paperwork. They were at camp, climbing a tree in their tutu which they know is a no-no," Tack says and a wave of relief comes over me as he makes one of his stupid jokes. "But they banged their arm. The nurse practitioner said they will be fine. Which is more than I can say for the nurse practitioner."

"What?"

"Well, after the exam the nurse said, 'Well, boys will be boys' and got an earful first from Jules and then from Evie about gender stereotyping. I refrained from punishing the poor guy any more." He laughs again and I can see the color even out in his face. "I've been in this place too long. I need to get out of here," he says.

"Let me get you home," I say. Tack's blond bangs are damp with sweat and matted against his forehead. I take my hand and move them back off of his face and he closes his eyes as I do it. When they open again I take his hand in mine and we walk out together.

Even though we have so much to say to each other we walk in silence almost all the way to the bridge back to New Hope. I've learned there are some things that can't be expressed in words. They can only be felt and experienced. With the bridge in sight, I take Tack's hand in mine again.

He doesn't say anything and neither do I. We walk hand in hand up the esplanade to the bridge's walkway like the only two people in the world.

He squints in the light of the setting sun, cocking his head just enough so that the taut skin on his neck stretches in a way that only Tack could make attractive.

"We need to talk. I found the book in my bag in New York."

Tack looks up at me. His eyes are soft and gentle, familiar and inviting. "I slipped it in there before you left. I wanted you to know how much it has meant to me over the years."

"Tack. Why didn't you tell me? How did you...? I thought the janitor threw it out or a possum made a nest out of it."

"No," he says with his eyes focused on me. "That's not what happened. I saw it there that day and yeah, I was an asshole, I walked past it when I knew it was for me and I just kept walking home with everyone from school and then it started to storm."

"I remember that. It was the first real hailstorm we ever had and the flash flooding. My mom got stuck."

"Right, well, I went back in the rain and the hail and I got the book. I've always had it. And I'll have you know I read it. All of it. More than a few times over the years. It's beautiful."

"You're beautiful," I say. "I thought you had forgotten about it. I thought you had forgotten me."

"I could never forget you. I should have showed you how important you were to me in high school. I couldn't do it then but I'm able to do it now." He puts his hand over mine.

"I'm sorry. I came back with all this bullshit attached to me. I thought I had to come back here and show you the person I've become. I should have told you I had planned to sell The Hideaway from the beginning but then everything changed and…"

"The Fourth of July?" he asks, his eyes searching mine.

"Yes. For you too?"

He nods and we both smile.

"I tried to fight it," I say. "But I knew once I got in your truck in Pittstown that it would take all of my strength not to fall for you again. When we kissed at the stream I thought that was the end of it. I would be able to get you out of my system."

Tack chuckles softly and the laughter goes straight into me through my heart. It almost makes me giggle. "I know it was silly to think I could sleep a few yards away from you and turn off everything I was feeling but then at the festival with Jules everything felt so right and I stopped resisting it."

"It felt like we were a family. I felt it too. I think Jules did also."

The mention of Jules makes me happy but also dispirited when I think about what kind of role model Tack must think I would be for them. "Tack, I should have told you the reason I bought the inn and that I was only planning to be here for the summer. I had opportunities to come clean but I was too caught up in feeling all these crazy things for you that I've been wanting to feel for so many years. I didn't want to spoil anything. I should have been honest with you. I know you raise Jules with openness and honesty. Are you sure you want someone like me to be part of that?"

"Vince," he says, shaking his head at me but still smiling. "For being the smartest person I know, sometimes your logic is pretty messed up. Don't you understand? In school you were your own person and that's what's important to me. That's why I liked you so much. Respected you more than anyone else I've ever known. Yes, I wish you had been more up front with me but I know your heart. I would be honored to have you share it with me and for us all to make a family."

The thought of being part of their family fills me with so much joy I think I might explode but I need to be sure this is what Tack wants. "I thought you didn't trust me and I thought you couldn't love me."

"I know I said that I didn't trust you but I was angry and hurt. I lost you once and the thought of losing you again made me lash out. But not being able to love you? You're wrong. Loving you is the easiest thing I've ever done. I've loved you ever since you wouldn't put your book down out by the fence. You think I stopped loving you when I kept my distance but it was the opposite."

"What do you mean?"

"The further and further you got from me the more I loved you deep in my heart. When you came back that dam just burst and the years of waiting just melted into a deeper connection."

He puts his hands on my cheeks and holds my head steady so we are looking right into each other's hearts.

"I love you, Vince."

The words.

He says them softly but they sound like trumpets ringing in my ear. I grab his hands and look into his eyes. "Tack, I love you. I've always loved you."

The setting sun melts into the river and orange and red streaks become purple and amber. In the distance I can see the inn and in front of it the last of the evening light dances across the water making a random path of sparkling diamonds. Tack's face glows in the soft pink light. He grabs my hand and turns toward me. I take my other hand and carefully brush a few stray bangs off his forehead. I linger on the view of his face for just a few seconds. In his eyes I see the guy I loved in high school but I also see the man I want to build my life with.

I tilt my head as he tilts his and our mouths melt into each other's.

I'm finally home.

Epilogue

Jules

"Come on," I yell. It feels like we have been waiting forever.

"Be patient, Jules. He'll be out as soon as he's ready," my dad says and goes back to the kitchen where he is making some pumpkin muffins that already smell incredible.

I run over to the window and look down Main Street. From the top floor of the inn, I can sort of see people already lining up on the street getting ready for the big race. It's hard to get a really good view because the new pride flags Vince bought are so huge.

I have the perfect pumpkin waiting for him on the table outside his and Dad's room. Then I think maybe Vince needs something sparkly so I run to my room and grab a purple feather boa that has some glitter on it. I wore it in the rain once so it looks a little funny but Vince won't care.

"The race is starting soon," I say and knock on their bedroom door. "Maybe you need more sparkle."

"I'm just about ready. I don't know how people walk in these things. Ouch," Vince says through the closed door.

Dad stops cooking and comes over to join me by the door. "On the count of three," he says. Then we both say, "One. Two. Three."

Vince opens the door, and I'm immediately stunned by how beautiful he looks. He is wearing a red sequined dress that I picked out from a thrift store in Doylestown, a long black wig like a witch but not scary, and the pair of high heels my dad bought him over the summer. He's wearing some smoky eye shadow and shiny lip gloss. He looks so pretty. I like the way his beard looks against the sequins which is weird because I hate the way it scratches when he hugs me. Today it looks good.

Vince walks toward us and he stumbles. My dad immediately goes to catch him so he doesn't fall over. "You look beautiful." Dad looks at Vince and they kiss. "Oh, and you taste like bubble gum."

"I loaned him my favorite gloss," I say to my dad. "But enough of the mushy stuff." I don't mind them kissing but they do it all the time and we have a race to get to.

"Vince," I say very seriously. "I've been going to this race since I was a baby. Right, Dad?"

"That's right," he says, smiling his goofy smile at me.

"So believe me: you want as big a pumpkin as you can

carry that's not too heavy. The small ones are hard to dec-orate and they just slip right out of your hands. Like Ms. Sanchez last year."

"Oh, yeah, from Paw Time. Barely made it past the start. Dropped her pumpkin and broke a heel before she got to the top of the hill. It was a real tragedy," Dad says.

From the window we can hear the race official calling participants. I stick my head out to make sure I can hear her. "We need all racers for the Twentieth Annual High Heels Drag Race to meet at the starting line at the bot-tom of Mechanic Street. The race is about to begin." I look down but it's hard to see around the waving pride flags that hang from the second floor. They almost take up the whole building. I move my head to catch a glimpse and I can see the crowd is getting bigger. There are men in dresses, women in tuxedos, men in tuxedos and women in dresses. Then there are a bunch of people who just look fabulous. I see Kevin and Evan without Paul and they see me and wave back. I look straight down and I see the top of Aunt Toula's head and then Anita. Anita's chair is deco-rated with silk flowers and streamers for the race. Then I see my mom with Ines, holding hands.

"Mom! Mom!" I scream so she can hear me over the crowd.

She looks up. "Jules! Get away from that window this instant or I am coming up there and taking you home."

"Fine," I say and close the window. I wasn't anywhere even close to falling out but that's Mom.

I grab Vince's hand. "Come on. Come on," I say but

he is so big it's hard to really move him when you are so much littler.

"Are you sure you are ready for this?" Dad asks Vince. He seems kind of worried about the answer.

"Ready? If you told me a year ago I'd be carrying a pumpkin racing up Mechanic Street in a wig, a dress and high heels, I would have told you you were out of your mind. But now I can't think of anything I want to do more, right here at home, with my family."

Vince's arm reaches for my dad to hug him and they start kissing.

Again.

* * * * *

Reviews are an invaluable tool when it comes to spreading the word about great reads. Please consider leaving an honest review for this or any of Carina Press's other titles that you've read on your favorite retailer or review site.

Jude rides a motorcycle, kisses hard and gives Iris the perfect distraction from her mess of a life. But come September, Iris is still determined to get out of this zero-stoplight town— unless Jude can give her a reason to stay.

Keep reading for an excerpt from The Girl Next Door *by* New York Times *bestselling author* Chelsea M. Cameron.

Chapter One

Iris

I smelled the ocean before I saw it. I took the long way back; the scenic route. Anything to prolong the inevitable. Turning my car onto a back road, I sighed as I rounded a corner and drank in the view of blue waves crashing over the rocky shore, coating the rocks and turning them dark. This was my home, whether I wanted to admit it or not. I'd started my life here in Salty Cove, and now I was back.

All too soon, I reached the turn for my parents' road. *My* road now. It took everything in me not to start crying when I pulled into the driveway and shut off the car. Time to face my new reality.

"We're here," I said to the snoring gray lump in a crate

in the backseat. "Can you please wake up and comfort me right now?"

With that, my Weimaraner, Dolly Parton, raised her head and blinked her sweet blue eyes at me.

"Thank you."

I got out of the car and went into the back to let her out of the crate. She jumped out and shook herself before sniffing the air.

"I know, you can actually smell the ocean here. It's not covered up by city smell. At least one of us will be happy with this situation."

Dolly started snuffling the ground and then found a spot to pee while I looked up at the house. Why did it look smaller? I hadn't been here for months and in that time, it had shrunk. The white paint peeled in places, and the flower boxes on the wraparound porch needed watering. I hoped the garden out back wasn't in as bad a shape.

The side door opened and out came my mother carrying a chainsaw. She didn't look at me immediately, but then she did and her face broke out into the most brilliant smile that made her look years younger.

"Hey, Mom," I said.

She put the chainsaw down on the porch before opening her arms. "Welcome home, baby girl."

I forced myself not to cringe at the nickname. I was twenty-two, hardly a baby at this point.

Still, I let myself be folded into her arms, and I drank in the familiar scent of fresh-baked bread and fresh-cut wood. She rubbed my back up and down and then leaned down to pet Dolly, who lost her shit and lapped up the attention.

"A tree came down last week, so I've been cutting it up. Come on in and see your father. You can bring your stuff in later. He's been antsy to see you all day."

I looked back at my car, which was packed to the roof with all the shit that I had left after I'd sold most of everything in a last-ditch attempt to cover my rent.

Mom put her arm around me and started filling me in on town gossip, but a loud rumbling distracted me. I turned my head in time to watch a sleek black motorcycle pull into the driveway next door.

"Is that—" I started to say, but then the rider got off the bike and pulled off their helmet, shaking out their short dark hair.

"Oh, yes, that's Jude. Her parents moved down to Florida and left her the house."

Jude Wicks. I hadn't seen her since she graduated four years ahead of me in school.

Jude didn't glance in my direction as she covered the bike, jogged up the steps, and slammed the front door of the house. I jumped at the sound.

Dolly whined and I looked down at her.

"Her parents left her the house?" I asked as Mom and I walked up the steps and into the house. We didn't have air-conditioning, so fans were doing all the work, just blowing around the semi-moist sea air.

Mom was distracted from answering by Dad yelling at her from his recliner. He'd hurt his back working for the power company for thirty-five years and was retired. They relied on Mom's income as a real estate agent and substitute teacher.

"Iris is here," Mom called to him.

"Baby girl!" he yelled when I came around the corner.

"Hi, Dad."

I went over to give him a huge hug. Dolly immediately put her chin in his lap and whined for attention.

"Hello, Dolly," Dad said with a chuckle, setting his coffee down next to a stack of library books beside his chair.

"What are you reading now?" I asked.

He held up the book he'd rested on the arm of the chair to keep his place. "Started reading these young adult books. This one's about these kids who are planning a heist to steal this magic stuff. You can have it when I'm done."

Mom poked her head in and asked me if I wanted some coffee. "Sure, thanks."

I sat down on the couch as Dolly curled up at his feet and closed her eyes.

Mom brought me a cup of black coffee and some creamer. I added enough so that the coffee turned from black to khaki. Perfect.

"How was your drive?" Mom asked.

We caught up on my trip, the fact that she'd cleared out my room for me, and what else was happening in town. Mostly it was about who my parents knew that had died, what they had died from, and talking shit about a few while simultaneously hoping they rested in peace.

Less than an hour at home and I already wanted to escape, but I was stuck here, at least for now.

I had to unpack my car, find a place for Dolly's food and water bowls, and settle into my room. Luckily for me, my brother, who was ten years older, had vacated it a long time ago to go to college.

My bed was small, but Mom had bought me a new mattress recently, so there was that. Still, it was a twin bed, when I'd been sleeping in a queen in my apartment. That had been left on the street. No one wanted someone else's mattress. The bed frame had been taken by Natalie, one of my former coworkers. I missed her already, and needed to text her that I'd made it home safe. She was so worried about me moving back to Maine that she'd literally bought me bear spray. I told her that the likelihood that I would die from a bear attack was slim to none, but she wouldn't listen.

The walls started to close in on me as I looked at the tiny bed. Sure, I'd had to share my old apartment with someone I didn't like, but my bedroom had been twice this size, and I'd had two big, beautiful windows that looked out on a courtyard filled with flowers and butterflies and twittering birds. Maine had all those things, but it wasn't the same.

To add insult to injury, none of my sheets or blankets were going to fit the bed. I added that to the list of things I needed to get with money I didn't have.

Dolly followed me into the room and climbed up on the bed. She took up most of it.

"I'm going to end up on the floor," I said to her. She closed her eyes and huffed out a sigh.

I sat on the edge of the bed and looked around. At least the posters I'd had on the walls in high school were gone, and the room was freshly painted white. My window looked out toward the ocean, which sparkled at me beyond a row of trees. At least I could see the ocean every day here.

My phone buzzed with yet another text. Natalie. I sent her a quick message that I'd arrived safe and had not been mauled by a bear. I ignored the message from Anna, my old roommate, about some dishes I'd apparently left behind and if it was okay for her to have them. Whatever. She could knock herself out. She'd stolen a bunch of my other shit, so I wasn't sure why she was contacting me about this. I considered blocking her number so I'd never have to speak to her again.

I reached out and stroked Dolly's velvet head. She leaned into my touch. "What are we gonna do?" I asked. She didn't answer.

Later that night, after I unpacked my car and had dinner that consisted of meatloaf, mashed potatoes, and a fiddlehead salad, I sat on the couch as Mom watched a reality talent show and Dad read.

This was my life now.

"What are your plans for tomorrow?" Mom asked during a commercial break.

"I'm not sure."

I hadn't thought any further than today. Everything else was a blank. I was always the girl with the plan, but now, I was adrift. An unmoored boat, lost at sea with no hope of rescue.

"I was talking to Cindy Malone the other day and they're hiring for summer help at The Lobster Pot," Mom said. "You did that in high school. I know she'd hire you. At least it would give you something during the summer until you can find something more permanent if you need to."

I tried not to make a face and instead grabbed one of the

books on Dad's "to be returned to the library" pile. Another young adult book; this time a Cinderella retelling. I read the blurb on the back and if I wasn't mistaken, it was a romance between two girls. I was surprised that my dad would want to read that. I wasn't going to comment, though. I cracked open the book and started to read. Mom still stood waiting for an answer.

"Oh, uh, sure. I'll call her tomorrow," I said.

I mean, what else was I going to do? Go down to the local bar and take up day drinking? Hang out at the gas station with the local teens? Sit on the beach with the tourists and get a horrible sunburn? I tried not to think about what I could be doing right now, if I was in Boston. Maybe dinner and drinks or pizza with my friends, a hot yoga class at my favorite studio, or even just taking a book to a coffee shop to read for a while and watch people pass on the street. If I wanted to have a professionally made cup here? I'd have to drive at least ten minutes and they definitely didn't have nondairy milk or know what a macchiato was.

Not that I could even afford a macchiato since I was fucking broke, and I needed money sooner rather than later. Working at The Lobster Pot was my best option.

"Sounds good, baby girl," Mom said with a smile. Her shoulders relaxed and she sat back in her chair. I realized she'd been worried. She seemed to be relieved I'd agreed to her plan so easily.

My parents and I hadn't really talked about what happened and why I was back, mostly because it wasn't for just one reason. There were many reasons, all culminating with me packing my shit in my car, loading up my dog, abandoning my friends, and driving back here.

I asked Mom if there was any ice cream in the freezer and she said that there was. While I was getting a spoon, I glanced out the window, which happened to look right into our neighbor's living room.

Jude.

The lights were on and she stood in the living room wearing nothing but a sports bra and some athletic shorts. The spoon I'd just grabbed clattered on the floor. As I stood up from retrieving the spoon, I found her staring directly at me. Instead of looking away like a normal person, I stared back.

Her hair had been long in high school and her arms hadn't been so...sculpted back then. At least not that I remembered. My mouth went dry and I held on to the spoon for dear life.

"What are you looking at?" a voice said behind me and I shrieked and dropped the spoon again. I turned around and found my mom leaning over my shoulder to see what I'd been staring at.

"Oh, nothing, just staring off into space." I rushed with my spoon and the ice cream back into the living room. My parents kept the room dark and the only light was from my dad's lamp and the TV, so I could hide in a corner with my lobster-red face.

What had come over me? I'd just stood there leering like a fucking creeper. Part of me expected a knock at the door and for her to storm in and ask what I'd been staring at.

That didn't happen, but it didn't stop me from looking up from my book every few minutes to check and make sure.

Before bed, I took Dolly out to do her business and my eyes kept flicking over to the house. The lights were still on, but I wasn't going to stare this time. I hadn't asked for more information from my mom about Jude, but I did wonder what she was doing back here. She'd hated this town, from what I remembered, so it couldn't just be because of her parents' house.

High school in a small town in Maine was brutal for anyone who didn't conform, and Jude had been adamant about not conforming. I'd done my best to get through, and the drama club had been my safe haven. I'd never thought seriously about acting after high school, since that was way out of my league, but I still thought about it every now and then. There was a community theater group a few towns away. Could I put myself out there and get into it again?

Dolly was taking her sweet time, sniffing the bushes at the edge of the porch to find the right one to pee near. I jumped as I heard a door slam, the door to the neighbor's house.

I froze with my back to the house, pretending I wasn't completely aware of what was happening. Was she leaving again on that motorcycle? Where would she go tonight? The only bar in town closed in less than an hour, and there was nothing else open. Unless she might be going to a friend's house for a party?

Or perhaps she was going to the beach for a midnight swim. I shivered at the thought of Jude slipping beneath the waves like a mermaid.

My ears perked for the rumble of the motorcycle starting up, but I didn't hear it. Dolly finally found her perfect spot and did her thing. She seemed content to sniff around the yard, so I let her, wrapping my arms around myself and breathing the sharp sea air. I'd missed this smell, even if I hadn't missed much else. Maybe I'd go for a midnight swim. The only danger of doing that in the height of the summer was encountering drunken teenagers, out having a bonfire on the beach and smoking a lot of weed.

I closed my eyes and took a few deep breaths before turning around. I told myself not to look at the porch next door, but my eyes had other ideas.

She was there, sitting on the porch on an Adirondack chair and staring out toward the ocean, just like I'd been doing. An open beer rested on the porch railing.

I swiveled my head away so she wouldn't catch me looking again, and at that moment Dolly decided that she'd make a mad dash for Jude's yard.

"Dolly!" I yelled as she bounded up the porch and went right for Jude. Well, shit. "Dolly, come back!"

She completely ignored me. I was going to have to go get her.

Groaning inside, I dragged myself over to the house, preparing for anything. What I found was Jude petting Dolly's head and Dolly closing her eyes in bliss and then trying to climb in Jude's lap.

"Dolly," I said, but she acted as if I wasn't even there. "I'm sorry. I should have kept her on the leash." I couldn't look up at Jude, so I watched her hands stroke Dolly's head.

The air around the porch seemed thicker somehow, or maybe it was just harder to breathe near Jude.

"It's okay," she said, and I felt like I'd never heard her voice before. I wasn't sure if I had. "I don't mind."

Dolly finally stopped trying to climb into the chair and settled for putting her paws and her head in Jude's lap.

"Sorry," I said again. I needed to take Dolly and get the hell out of here, but I couldn't move. My feet were glued to her porch.

"Haven't seen you in a while, Iris," she said. Her voice had a rough quality that made me think of bar smoke and darkness. There was a hard quality about her that made my stomach flip over a few times.

"Yeah, I moved back today." My gaze finally crept its way up to her face only to find her watching me with fathomless brown eyes. Her face was all sharp angles, along with her haircut. A fluttering in my stomach erupted, and I forgot what we were talking about until she blinked again.

"When did you get back?" My voice trembled, and I hoped she didn't hear it.

Her fingers danced back and forth on Dolly's head. "Last year," she said, but didn't elaborate. Chatty.

"I should probably go," I said, stating the obvious.

"Stay if you like," she said, picking up her beer and gesturing to the empty chair next to her.

"Okay?" I collapsed into the chair and tried to calm my galloping heart.

"Do you want a beer?" she asked after a few seconds of silence.

"No, thank you." What was I doing here? I should have

grabbed Dolly and run back into the house. Was Jude doing this so she could confront me about staring at her earlier?

I had no idea how to have a conversation with her so I stopped trying to think of things to say and just sat there, my insides twisting around like pissed-off snakes. At least Dolly was enjoying herself.

Jude didn't seem eager to say anything either, so there we were. I kept expecting my mom to open the door and yell for me to come back. At least that would give me an escape route.

Out of the corner of my eye, I watched Jude. She petted Dolly with one hand and the other lifted the beer to her lips periodically. She wore a T-shirt and the same shorts as earlier.

I needed to stop thinking about that earlier non-outfit. I blushed hard and hoped she couldn't see in the dark.

If I strained my ears, I could just barely hear the crash of the waves. Somewhere nearby, a soft boom followed by another let me know someone was setting off fireworks.

"That's a cool motorcycle," I blurted out, and wished I could walk into the ocean and disappear.

"Thank you. It's not very useful in the winter, but it's good for getting around in the summer." She pressed her lips together as if she'd said too much.

"I've never been on a bike. I'm scared I'd fly off or something." This kept getting worse and worse.

"I'm sure you'd be fine, once you tried it. Do you always let fear dictate your life?"

I sat up, shocked. "*No*," I said, but it didn't sound convincing. "You don't even know me." I didn't know her either, but I was the one being called out.

"True. Just something to think about." She moved Dolly's head and stood up. "See you later," she said, and went into the house, leaving me and Dolly wondering what the hell had just happened.

Dolly came over to me and whined.

"Let's go home," I said and she seemed to understand me. I got up with shaking legs and made my way back to the house. The lights were still on next door when I glanced back one more time.

Chapter Two

Jude

I tried to remember her, but since there had been four years between us in high school, the memories were hazy. She'd had friends, from what I'd seen, and seemed to do okay in that fishbowl environment. Not always fighting against the current like me.

I didn't know what she was doing back here, and I was trying not to care, but this was one of the first interesting things to happen in Salty Cove in a while. I also hadn't missed the way she'd looked at me earlier. Might be my imagination, but I was pretty sure I'd seen interest there, which was interesting on its own. She'd definitely been interested in guys, last I knew. I'd known that I liked girls, and girls only, from a young age. I'd refused to hide who I was and had come out at an age where kids were the most vicious. Still, I'd gotten through it but bore the hidden scars.

Not that I was going to pursue anything with her, even if she was interested. No, I wasn't ready, even now. It had been more than two years but not much had changed. Living in Salty Cove and fishing for lobster was like living in a space where time barely passed, where it moved so slow that you didn't notice and suddenly you were old and still living the same life you'd had for dozens of years, even though you swore you wouldn't. This town locked you in, made you forget that there was anything or anyone outside it.

I should probably get out more, but look what getting out of Maine had gotten me. I was back to the place I never wanted to be and I didn't have any plans about leaving. Where would I go? I'd lost everything. I was lucky to have parents who were thrilled that they could stop paying a property manager and get free labor from their daughter. Now they could spend their time soaking up the sun and drinking cocktails every afternoon in Florida. If I could stand to be with them, I might have joined them.

No, I don't think I could handle living in Florida. I wasn't really handling living here, but it was easier to float through my life in a familiar environment, even if that environment was so homogenous that everyone was related to everyone else. Except for me.

My thoughts drifted from my life here back to Iris. She'd clearly gone off to college and now she was back. I knew her father had retired with some injuries, so maybe that was why. Or maybe it was something else and she'd needed a soft place to land. This town was a safety net for so many people. She seemed a little frenetic, or maybe that was her personality. Nervousness radiated from her in waves. It didn't bother me, though, which was surprising. I normally gravitated toward people who were like me, reserved and quiet, but if she was going to be next door for a while, maybe we could hang out. I definitely needed more friends, since I didn't have anyone close, just acquaintances.

I'd touched on a nerve when I'd told her not to live in fear, but I'd done that on purpose to see what would happen. Chalk it up to boredom.

She was cute too, I'd have to give her that much. Wide-set blue eyes that had untold stories behind them underneath light brown curls. Her curves were generous and lush. No, I wasn't going to think about her body. Completely inappropriate. I hadn't thought about anyone's body *that* way since...

Everything always came back to that. To *her*. I couldn't even think her name without a stab to my heart.

If Iris was cute was irrelevant because I wasn't going to love anyone ever again. I'd done it once and once was enough. I'd gambled and lost, big time. Iris probably wasn't going to come back anyway, because I'd been rude and had just left her on the porch with her dog. I'd been afraid that she was going to start asking me personal questions, or try to talk to me, and I was out of practice talking to other people. That was the best part of my job: the no talking to anyone. Sure, there was the stink of bait and the hard physical labor, but every day when I went out, I got to be alone. I preferred being alone these days. It hadn't always been like that, and I still had friends who tried to get in touch every now and then. Some were persistent and kept trying, even when I gave them nothing. I guess there was something to be said for that. Too bad I was such a shitty friend. Maybe I could practice with Iris.

I finished my beer inside and put the TV on so the house wasn't so silent. I didn't really watch it, but the noise and color distracted my brain for a little while. Due to my job, I'd adjusted to a different sleep schedule, so after I put the bottle in the recycling, I stripped off my clothes and headed to bed. I lay with the windows open and the sound of the ocean doing its best to lull me to sleep.

My eyes closed and I felt myself float toward sleep on a soft current. It only lasted for a minute as my brain conjured her face and then I was wide-awake and trying not to cry. They weren't nightmares, exactly, but they did keep me from ever getting a good night's sleep. Most of the time my job exhausted me so much that my body would sort of shut down anyway and I'd take a nap or two in the afternoon, but for the most part, I didn't sleep.

After trying about six different sleeping positions, I got up and grabbed a blanket to sit with on the couch. I was learning how to crochet, which kept my hands busy and my mind thinking about stitches and counting and making sure I didn't leave a hole. I was testing out different techniques on squares, and eventually I'd put them all together as a blanket. At least, that was the plan. I was only on the second square, and my squares didn't exactly look like the pictures, but at least I was doing something. I'd burned through so many hobbies in the last two years, including puzzles, wire jewelry, baking bread, and raising succulents, to keep myself sane. Barely.

I curled up on the couch for a few hours of rest before my alarm went off. It was still dark when I got up and got dressed. I kept my regular wardrobe separate from my work wardrobe. I had to. You could never get the stink of bait out of jeans, let me tell you. I actually kept my work clothes on the porch so they didn't funk up the house. I tossed my extra jacket, boots, and oil pants in a bag on the back of my bike, packed up some protein bars and a sandwich, coffee, and water for the day, sucked down a protein shake, and I was ready for work. My bag was already packed with the other essentials: sunblock, a hat, gloves, a portable charger for my phone, and a few tampons. Just in case.

I spared one glance for the house next door, but the lights were all off, since most normal people weren't awake at this hour. At first, it had been horrible, waking before the sun. Now I relished this quiet. I often spent entire days where I only had to communicate in a few words or grunts. That probably wasn't healthy, but it was working for me right now.

I headed down to the wharf to grab my dinghy and row out toward my boat. I wasn't alone, and shared a few nods and waves and grunts with my fellow cohorts. There weren't a whole lot of women on the water, but the guys had never really said much to me. I was sure they had talked behind my back, but no one said anything to my face. Not that I would have put up with any bullshit from them. I'd been telling men off my entire life and needed more practice.

My shoulders popped and cracked as I rowed out to my boat, named the *June Marie*. I'd bought it from a man who had named it for his wife and daughter, as many did, and I hadn't been able to come up with a better name, so I kept it. Maybe one of these days I'd change it to something like the *Salty Bitch*, but then that would mean I was staying here and the boat was mine and this was my life now. I didn't want this to be my life. I used to picture my life in so many different ways, and now it was a blank. I was stuck, but I couldn't find the way forward. I wanted to dream again. I just didn't know how. Back in the day, I'd planned on getting my MBA and then opening a coffee shop or a greenhouse or a bar. I didn't know what my business would be. I just knew that I wanted to work for myself, and that seemed like the way to do it. I'd been young and naïve then.

The *June Marie* roared to life and I steered it out of the harbor. The first few days like this on the water had been spent acclimating to the waves and the up-and-down motion of the boat, but somehow, my body had stopped fighting it and I wasn't puking over the side while trying not to hit a buoy or a seal.

I always played music on the boat, so I turned on my favorite playlist. Lizzo blasted from the small speakers I'd rigged up in the cabin. It was cold as fuck today, so I wrapped myself up and sucked down half of my thermos of coffee as the sun rose. The forecast was for temps in the eighties later, a rarity for Maine. Right now the air was downright frosty. That wasn't something I had bargained on when I started. I'd learned a lot since then. A bunch of the guys I'd hung out with in high school had worked for their dads, and I'd helped out once or twice, so I wasn't completely new to fishing. I'd still had to fumble my way through at first.

I reached my first buoy, which was painted white with a black stripe around the middle. I hadn't been very creative there, I had to admit. I set about the nasty job of throwing bait into bags to re-bait the trap, and then the business of hauling the trap up from the ocean floor. If I wasn't such a small operation (only fifty traps), I might have had help in the form of a sternman, but then I would have had to talk to someone, and that would have been the worst. I'd rather curse and struggle and take longer doing things on my own than hire someone else. Plus, I'd have to pay them and I was barely making it work as it was. At least I didn't have to pay a mortgage.

I lost myself in the rhythm of my work: bait, haul trap, pull out lobsters, measure, rubber band, re-bait, toss back in ocean.

By the time most people were getting up for work, I was almost halfway through my traps for the day. I had two rotations and alternated them every other day. My body had grown used to the physical work, but I would never get used to the smell of bait and diesel. No amount of showers seemed to remove the smell. Guess that was another bonus of having a sternman: someone else got to do the stinky jobs.

I had a decent haul and headed back to the lobster pound, where they'd buy the lobsters right from the boat, boil them in the restaurant upstairs, and serve them all in the same day. I also threw a few in a cooler on the back of the bike for myself, since it was cheaper than buying organic chicken at the grocery store.

I hosed myself off near the dock and decided to head home instead of hanging out to shoot the shit with the other lobstermen. Sometimes I lurked and they let me hang on the edges of their conversations, listening but not contributing. They didn't seem to mind, since we were all in the trenches together. I could have joined if I wanted to, but I'd never tried and the longer I didn't try, the harder it became.

I stopped quickly to fuel up the bike and grab a fresh-baked croissant and another huge black coffee at the only gas station in town. It was also a variety store, stocking everything from guns to gummies to wedding gowns. Seriously. I didn't know who was buying said gowns, but they had them anyway.

The lobsters went into the fridge out back before I stripped completely and ran for the shower. I honestly didn't care if the neighbors saw me dashing through the house after I abandoned my clothes in the doorway. I didn't used to, anyway. Maybe now I should care a little bit about a certain neighbor seeing me completely naked. No, I wasn't going to think about that. I wasn't going to think anything. I was just going to close my eyes and try and wash off the smell of dead fish guts and also not think about anything at all. Nothing. I wanted to think nothing.

I wanted to *be* nothing.

Don't miss The Girl Next Door *by Chelsea Cameron,*
out now from Carina Adores.
www.CarinaPress.com

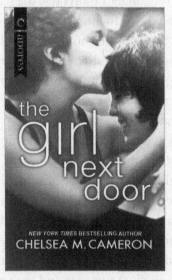
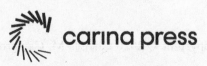